A NOVEL

INFERNO
ROAD

BESTSELLING AUTHOR
K. LUCA

EBook ISBN: 978-1-958445-13-6

Paperback ISBN: 978-1-958445-14-3

Hardback ISBN: 978-1-958445-15-0

Cover Design by Pretty In Ink Creations

Editing and Proofreading by My Brother's Editor

INFERNO ROAD

K. LUCAS

For my son

"Once more into the fray,
into the last good fight I'll ever know.
Live and die on this day.
Live and die on this day."

(The Grey, 2011)

ONE

A glance at the clock on the dash tells me I've been sitting on this freeway for over forty-five minutes, and another through the windshield says I'm still not halfway home. I let go of the steering wheel as I stretched. *What a great day to be sitting in traffic, Ben.*

I start to ease up on the break as the car in front inches forward, but as I do, the driver in the next lane swerves into the opening, leaving half his car blocking both lanes. With a curse, I slam my foot back on the brake pedal and my hands on the wheel, this close to an accident. A few other cars honk and all I can do is stare at the other driver who's doing anything to avoid my gaze through his windshield.

Made it far there, buddy, didn't you? We're not even moving. What the hell were you t—

The music on the radio stops. "Thank you for listening to Seattle's Rock Station! We're here with our special guest, Tim Howard, the volcanologist who warned us all about Rainier. Tim, It's the five-year anniversary of the eruption, have you noticed any—" The DJ starts droning on and on, but I'm not in the mood to listen. There's nothing worse than listening to people gab on and on, when all I want is some good music while I try to get home in one piece.

As I turn the tuner knob, trying to get hold of my temper, I think about my wife and kids at home. Rachel is probably making dinner or getting ready to. I'm usually always home by this time; not being there feels so odd. *I shouldn't be here*. If I wouldn't have agreed to the overtime, I'd be at home already.

My eyes drift to the clock again as if it's a magnet that won't fully release me. "It's Thursday. Ryan's still at practice," I say to myself. "She's going to have to pick him up —unless he got a ride from someone...Bea could be helping her to make things go a little faster." When I texted earlier to say I'd be late, we didn't exactly go into specifics about the kids.

My stomach rumbles as the tuner finally lands on a good station. *That's more like it!* I smile as Metallica's "Enter Sandman" flows through my speakers. With a sigh, I lean back in my seat and relax as much as possible. I've still got a long way to go this evening, but if I'm going to battle traffic, at least give me some of my favorite bands.

The memory of today—of work, my boss, the meeting, everything going wrong, the office politics, all of it— finally starts to fade a little. *None of it matters, Ben*, I remind myself, trying to erase the memory. Part of me has always been glad for the long commute, glad that even though I'm forced to work in the big city, I can still drive home to a small town and leave it all behind where it came from.

Days like today are nothing but bad news, and dwelling on them doesn't do me any damned good. So what if I had to stay late? So what if I hit a little traffic?

The cars ahead start to inch forward again. I watch as the driver, who cut me off moments ago, straightens the car out and comes to a dead stop once again.

My phone rings, and I look at the caller ID before answering. "I was just thinking about you cooking me a delicious dinner."

"You were, were you?" Rachel says. "Well, I was calling to see if you'd pick up something on your way home."

"Might be another hour yet. Traffic is worse than normal."

"That's okay. Ryan isn't home yet. I'll call in an order at—" Rachel's voice cuts off.

"Rach?" I look at my phone to see nothing but a black screen. The call dropped. The music on the radio turns to static. *Great, just what I need now.* I slap the radio to shut it off and redial Rachel.

Two beeps ping in my ear.

Call failed.

My eyes dart up to my service bars—no signal. *What the hell?*

I rest my phone back in its spot inside my cupholder and turn the radio back on. There's still nothing but static playing, so once again, I twist the tuner dial. *Even listening to talking is better than this...*

Out the window, other drivers seem to all be doing the same thing—all reaching for their phones and radios.

The sight sends chills down my spine. I look out the other side and my rearview mirror—all the same. People confused, on the verge of panic even. Some are arguing, others looking around, just like me.

Something isn't right here.

Horns start blaring. Drivers are beginning to roll down their windows and yell, either demanding others to move or asking what the hell's going on. Hands and fists and fingers are in the air. On the horizon, there's nothing but tail lights. "There's an accident or something. No one is going anywhere, people."

A few drivers get out of their cars to investigate. Moments later, more follow. For a split second, I consider joining them. This isn't the first traffic jam I've been in—not even close. But there's something that doesn't sit right with me here.

Since when does the phone signal cut out on a major freeway just outside one of the largest cities in America? Since when does nothing but static play on the FM radio when I'm not in a dead zone? Normally we'd at least be inching a bit at a time, but now there's no movement at all. Drivers are shutting off their engines to save gas because we're not even snails at this point.

I grab my phone to try Rachel again. Still no signal.

There's nothing to do but sit and wait until whatever this is passes—and it will. It always does. Or satisfy my curiosity by getting out of the truck and going for a walk in the middle of the freeway. I consider it but decide I'm curious, just not *that* curious, at least not yet.

About twenty minutes pass before something in the distance catches my attention. The people walking—the ones who'd gotten out of their vehicles—they're running.

They're running back the way they'd come. Some are waving their hands in the air, screaming something unintelligible, others are crying. A few heads clear off the road and into the nearby forest.

"What the hell is going on?" I say as if someone might actually give me an answer. My chest feels tight as dread works its way to my gut.

I see it then.

The horizon lights up like a candle—red and orange and yellow. A ball of fire rising into the air. There's no time to think, to take in what was happening, let alone *do* anything about it. The blast wave sails toward me faster than my brain can process. One after another, cars flip over, glass breaks, trees fall. The sound catches up to it then—a deafening blast that brings tears to my eyes.

Then my world goes black.

TWO

THIS MORNING

There's something about the alarm clock this morning, screaming in my ear, relentless, over and over and over, that makes me rip it from the wall and throw it across the room. It's something I often *want* to do but never follow through with because that's not something rational, normal people usually do when they first wake up. But today, I do do it, and I do it without even thinking about it.

Rachel startles at the sudden sound of plastic smacking the dresser, most likely one or both of them cracking. She distances herself from me automatically, a knee-jerk reaction.

Reaching up to rub the sleep from my eyes, I take in a deep breath. *It's just one of those days—already.* I'd give anything to roll over next to her, snuggle beneath the blankets, and go right back to sleep. But I can't do that. It's not in the cards.

As I stand, Rachel's voice, still husky with sleep, asks, "Are you okay?"

"Fine," I answer, moving to the bathroom. I hate that

for even a minute, she was scared of me. Maybe not on a conscious level, but it was ingrained into her cells to move away from me.

Was the alarm really that terrible? I had to teach it a lesson it wouldn't forget. I'll admit—it felt good as hell to chuck that damned thing, but I'm in too bad a mood to be able to enjoy the feeling.

It's going to be a bad day. I can tell already. The alarm clock makes me want to gouge my eyes out, snapping at my wife, and now I have to get ready for a meeting I don't want to be a part of.

Get a damn hold of yourself, Ben! I take a moment to stare at myself in the mirror, my eyes boring into their own reflection as if I could glimpse my own soul. *You are an adult. Act like one.*

I should go back through the doorway and apologize to Rachel. I need to tell her sorry we started the day on the wrong foot, and I'll make her a kick-ass cup of coffee while she showers. I allow myself a few minutes before stepping back into the bedroom, and—she's gone.

"Rach?"

Voices come from the hallway. The kids are up. The day has started. Too late.

I'll talk to her later. I make it a point on my long list of items to *not forget to do* and move into get-ready-for-work mode.

A quick shower and shave later, I'm staring at the clothes in my closet with growing dread. "Rach!" I call.

Where the hell is it?

It's so stupid. So insignificant in the scheme of things. But today is just not my fucking day.

The suit I bought, specifically for today, the only suit I own that fits me since I've gained twenty pounds, and the only one I plan on buying until I *lose* that said twenty—isn't here. I call it my power suit because it makes me feel like a badass and because I *need* to feel like a badass if I'm going to make it through this meeting in one piece. It's a tool for my mental arsenal, and not seeing it here, clean and pressed—like I prepared *last week*—sends me into semi panic mode.

"Rachel!" I call for my wife again, stepping out of the closet, into the bedroom, then calling again in the hallway.

Where the hell is she?

"What's wrong?" she answers from inside Bea's room.

I go to the doorway, watching her dress our daughter for kindergarten. Bea squints as Rachel brushes her hair, holding tight at her temple in an attempt not to tug too hard. "Have you seen my new suit?" I ask.

"It should be in the closet."

"Yeah, it *should* be, but it's not."

She looks up at me. "Are you accusing me of taking your suit, Ben?"

"No—I'm just asking if you know where it is. I've really got to get going."

"Can you wear one of your others?"

The question sends me off the edge. I storm back down the hallway to the bedroom, knowing if I stand there and respond, I'll argue with her for the next hour. *Can I wear another one?* Well, I think the twenty pounds I put on my gut would have something to say about that.

She knows it too. She knows how I feel about it, and not only that but how not being able to fit in any clothes you own can really suck. I'm not going to buy a new wardrobe, either, although I'm sure she would love the opportunity to take me shopping for one.

Back in the closet, I start pulling hangers from the rail, tossing clothes into a pile on the floor. When half the closet lies there, it's clear the suit isn't here. It's not stuck between shirts or shoved in the back in an awkward position. It's gone.

I check the time on my watch.

Shit.

"Okay. It's fine. I'll be fine without it."

What does a power suit matter anyway? Obviously, I have other clothes to wear to work. I won't look or feel as good, but I'll get over it. One of the biggest meetings of my career will go well based on my merit, not my appearance, right?

Right.

Moving faster now that I'm running late, I shuffle through the clothes on the floor to pick out the best shirt and slacks I can. The shirt fits fine, the pants a little snug around the waist, but I should be able to sit in them for hours on end without too much discomfort.

As I'm finally ready to leave the bedroom, Rachel comes back. "Did you find it?" she asks.

"Does it look like I found it?" I scowl down at the clothes I'm wearing.

"You look nice."

"I feel like crap."

"You'll do great." She grabs hold of my hand. "I'm sorry about the suit."

"You're sure you don't know where it is?"

She steps back, frowning. "Do you really think I'd hide it from you? I know how important today is to you."

"I just don't know where the hell it could be!"

"Well, neither do I. I'm tired of being the one blamed when you can't find something."

"I'm not blaming you."

"That's exactly what you're doing."

I look back down at my watch. I'm so late now, even speeding isn't going to do anything. *Just perfect.* "I have to go," I say. I pull her into a quick hug, the only way I know how to tell her I love her and I'm sorry for being in such a foul mood without saying the words. Five minutes later, I'm in my truck, backing out of the driveway.

THREE

The parking lot is full. *Why are there so many cars here today?* It's never this packed, with every spot filled and people forced to park either along the curb or down the road at the public parking lot.

I'm also never this late. In fact, I'm usually early to work and often get one of the first-row spots.

Any other day, this would be no big deal. Any other day, I'd laugh about it and smile at my colleagues as I walk off the elevator. Today though, my nerves are shot.

Sweat pours off me, drenching the armpits of my shirt. I turn the wheel toward an open space, stopping when I see the car is double parked. There's no choice but to go down the road a block to the public lot.

One eye remains glued to my watch as I step off the elevator, heading straight for the meeting room. When I step inside, all eyes turn to me, one by one drifting to my sweat stains and disheveled appearance. Beet red, I slip through the back of the room toward the nearest open chair, but my boss isn't going to let me off that easy.

"Nice of you to join us, Ben," he says from the head of the table.

"Thanks, George. Nice to be here."

"A little trouble with the alarm this morning?"

To my chagrin, my flush deepens. The only thing I can do is plaster a fake grin to my face as I stare around the room full of high-ranking CEOs, board members, and upper management while George draws attention to me rather than get on with the damned meeting. *If he only knew how right he was about the alarm, he'd laugh.*

"A little traffic." I nod my assent, adding, "I'm ready to present. Shall I—"

"No, that's quite alright. Shay can handle it from here."

There's nothing I can do but sit back and watch as Shay takes the information I've worked on gathering day and night, sweat and bled for, for the last month, and presents it as his own. He's articulate, good-looking, put together, and he was here on time, ready to take over the minute George needed.

Nausea builds in my stomach as I watch the way the higher-ups nod and engage with him. A few even take notes on the information. "Well done, Shay. Thank you."

The CEO shakes his hand and *winks*. A subtle nod to George and on to other topics.

Shay's eyes flick to mine for a brief moment, the only indication he understands what just happened.

It's fine, I tell myself. *I'll just have to be on time next time. No —not just on time. Early, and wearing my suit.* My mind drifts off focus, imagining myself going to the gym, not only losing that damned twenty pounds but gaining a little lean muscle as well. Maybe the next time I'm sitting here in front of these people, they won't recognize me. They won't remember the schmuck who walked in late, and maybe, I won't even need that suit because I'll be smoother than glass all on my own.

"Ben? Are you with us?" George says a little too loudly.

I blink. "Yeah, boss."

"Good." He leans back in his chair, smiles, and asks. "Then, what do you say?"

Shit.

"Didn't catch that last question."

Laughter.

"If you weren't such a good analyst, Ben," George says, winking.

It takes all my willpower not to cringe.

I force myself to take a late lunch. While I sit in the cafeteria, staring at the TV, my mind wanders again to the next time I'll have an opportunity to prove myself.

At this point, I'm worried if I threw up my hands and looked for another job, I'm not sure how good a reference George would be. *But is it worth the effort to keep trying to make him see me?*

It seems like there's something about me he just doesn't like, or there's just something about Shay that he likes better, and no matter what I do, it's always going to be there. I'm okay with not being the favorite, but I'm not okay with being treated like a pile of shit that he stepped in. That promotion was *mine.* I worked for it. I earned it. I deserve it.

And then I showed up to one of the most important meetings of my career—late...and drifted off while my boss was talking.

The news on the television draws my attention. *An intoxicated man near the town of Welldeer was arrested for a bomb threat when he entered a gas station late at night, harassing patrons. The attendant said when no one offered to give any money, the man threatened to "blow everyone to hell."*

Welldeer. That's my town. Wow, scary to think things like that can happen so close to home.

I check the time again—wouldn't want to be late getting back to the grind—and send Rach a quick text.

> Did the kids make it to school okay?

> Yes. How was the meeting?

> It was shit. Talk later.

Refusing to be late again today, I come back from lunch early. It's not like I have a habit of being late anyway, but after this morning, I want to double my efforts at proving myself. I want to be at my computer, being productive, anytime George looks my way.

An hour later, I'm in the middle of my next project when George walks off the elevator, slapping Shay's back. They're about to coast right past my desk when George stops in front of me. "Need you to stay late tonight, Ben. You don't mind, do you?"

Yes, I do mind, actually. "Would you mind if I stay tomorrow instead? Tonight is—"

George turns to Shay, smiling. "You see, Shay, this is exactly why I appreciate you. Your willingness to go the extra mile for a job that needs to get done."

"It's my pleasure, boss. This place is better than home, anyway," Shay says, laughing at his own stupid joke.

This place is definitely not better than home, and no, I don't want to be here any longer than I have to be. Maybe George sees that, and it's what he hates about me. But I *do* want to be valued as an employee, and I do understand the need to go over and above sometimes. I can't blame him for favoring an employee who works harder. It's up to me to prove that I can and *will* work just as hard as Shay.

"I'll stay," I say. "Whatever you need me to do, George. I'm the man."

"Excellent." He turns back to Shay as they walk away. "I told you he'd cover for you. Now, what time should we make reservations for? Around six?"

I'm an idiot.

Rachel is going to have to find one of the other parents to bring Ryan home from practice today since I won't be able to pick him up now. I'm also going to hit rush-hour traffic on the way home. What was that feeling I had this morning? I *knew* today was going to suck.

I close my eyes, wishing it was Friday, then wishing I could call in sick tomorrow, knowing I can't. *I should.* I should go home right this second, I should up and quit.

Maybe I should. But I'm not going to.

FOUR

NOW

I open my eyes to a sheet of black. My head aches worse than I can remember in my life, worse even than my most painful hangover during college. I start to lift a hand to my temple, but something's off. My arm is heavier than usual, and I feel out of balance. I blink, trying to clear my vision, and that's when I realize I'm upside down.

It comes back to me—the gridlock, the people running on the blacktop, the explosion. *If it's night now, it means I've been out for hours.* An image of Rachel comes to mind, worried, glued to the news. Would she know what's going on?

The memory of our argument from earlier in the day haunts me. *I should've just let it go.* Why did I have to keep nagging her like that? I knew all day long that I should've just texted her to apologize. Should've just sucked up my pride and got it over with, but instead, I continued on like nothing happened in the first place.

What she must've been thinking when I asked her about dinner.

I'm going to get the hell out of here, and the minute I see her, I'm going to say sorry. Not just for the stupid argument but for not saying sorry in the first place and then for pretending it didn't happen. *God, what a day this has been.* From the time I woke up until now, it's been a shit show. *I can't wait to see what the rest of the day has in store.*

I try to turn in my seat to get a better view of the outside, but it's a struggle. The seatbelt must've locked when the truck flipped because there was no slack for me to move. When I look around, everything is dark besides the narrow yellow and orange glow through the corner of the windshield.

Something's on fire out there. The burning smell is undeniable and at the strength of it, and the sweat pouring off my body—I'm wondering if the truck isn't on fire too. *This is bad. This is very fucking bad. I have to get out of here.*

Bracing myself for a fall, I feel for the seat belt button, push it, and drop. I grit my teeth against the pain of broken glass in my hands and arms as I try for the door. It takes me a few seconds to find the handle. I push—but it's stuck. I shove harder, but it's still no use.

I scramble to turn on the cab lights—anything to help me see what's going on. Once I have them on, I almost choke at the sight surrounding me. *My god, I'm lucky to be alive.* The passenger side door is caved in, and the back of the truck is worse—it's missing. Gone. The remnants of the tailgate look like an accordion, nearly touching the back of my driver's seat.

For a moment, it hits me that maybe I'm dead. I'm sitting here in an impossible situation, killed by whatever blast happened earlier. I'm just a spirit, stuck here forever now, doomed to wonder what happened to me for the rest of eternity.

Rachel's face flashes before me again, along with my kids. My family. My life. Did they wind up making dinner after all? Did they give up waiting on me? Of course they did. Rach wouldn't send the kids to bed hungry, and she wouldn't keep them up past their bedtime on a school night.

She's going to live the rest of her life remembering me bitching about something stupid that doesn't even matter. She's going to remember me never apologizing, not just for whatever was said today, but for all the times I never said sorry. It'll grow over the years into resentment toward me—maybe even something stronger.

She might remember some of the good times, the love we share, but bad memories always come back to the surface. They always trump happy ones. And the memory of today, *how* I die, will stay with her. She'll wind up hating me.

I see her pacing the house, checking her phone as the hours pass. "I hate that you have to commute so far," she always says.

"There's a price to pay for life in a small town," I always remind her. We love where we live, but we still have to work, and that means commuting.

Why couldn't I just listen to her?

Would she see the news of a pileup on social media? *No, this wasn't just a pileup.* Whatever happened is a hell of a lot worse than that. It was a ball of fire in the sky, like nothing I'd ever seen. That sound—goose bumps break out on my arms. My ears still ring from the roar. I never want to hear anything like that again in my entire existence.

The memory brings me back to reality. I'm not dead. The dead have no fear. I'm alive, and my family is still waiting for me, and I'm sure as shit afraid.

I have to get moving. Get the hell out of this truck. The longer I sit here, the more danger I'm in. The smell of smoke is getting stronger, along with the sound of burning. I don't have long before my truck joins the inferno—if it's not on fire already.

I reach for the center console, and with a little effort, I'm able to pry it open. Desperate for anything that might help, I shuffle through the contents. A few fast-food napkins, a pen, some gum, and loose change, are all I can find.

"Come on!" I cry, slamming the lid shut.

My palms are growing damp as my eyes scan the rest of the cab. I eye the seat I just fell from, then zone in on the headrest. A memory of a specific TV show comes back to me. They did this—trapped someone in a car and showed how to get out. My heart falters as I reach for the headrest.

For a frantic moment, nothing happens. I yank harder. My damp hands slip against the leather. "Come on, you fucking thing!" I yell, adjusting my hands for a better grip. When it still doesn't budge, I finally stop, take another look, and realize I could slap myself. I wasn't pressing in the release tab.

I press it in now and pull the headrest clear out of the seat. When it's out, I eye the metal bars with a mixture of hope and doubt. "Please let this work," I whisper. Then I reach back and slam the metal against the driver's side window.

Cracks branch out across the glass like a spider's web. I pull back again and with renewed hope, bring the metal poles of the headrest down against the glass over and over, until I finally break through. As smoke pours in, I pull myself out.

FIVE

My feet land on dirt instead of pavement, and rather than being met with cool night air, I'm almost suffocated by heat and flame. One look tells me I've been thrown clear from the road, about a hundred yards from the freeway. The truck landed wedged between two pines just on the outskirts of the forest. The ground is littered with debris from the blast, but most importantly, the freeway is on fire.

The flames are so hot the blacktop is borderline melting. Paint is boiling on the surface of cars, and the heat radiating even from this distance is enough to make me take a few more steps backward. I look through the flames, straining to see or hear anyone, but there's no movement.

"Hello?" I call, trying not to choke. *There has to be someone. I can't be the only one.*

No one answers, so I try again. "Hello!"

Even with the sight I'm faced with, I call until my throat goes raw. *There has to be someone. There has to be.*

My head spins as I attempt to make sense of the situation and acclimate to my surroundings. I may have been passed out for hours, but to my conscious mind, five minutes ago, this was a regular road full of cars and *living* humans. Now, it's a disaster area, void of life.

I start moving along the perimeter of the forest, as close to the heat as I dare. It's the only light I have, and I'm not sure if it's a good or bad thing that it's bright enough to light my way. There are other cars and trucks that were blown off the road too, some crumpled into tin cans against tree trunks, others flipped just like my truck was, and one is even up *in* the trees.

It doesn't take me long to reach a green sedan, flipped, one side completely caved in. From the look of it, I already know what I'll find, but I have to see for myself. I lean down to check inside. Two people are dead in the front seats.

I stumble back, almost tripping over scattered car parts. Another truck is near—surely they would've—

I stop in my tracks when I'm close enough to see a man's head sticking out of the windshield. Glass is protruding from his face and his eyes—open eyes, staring at me. They hold me in place, frozen, and all I can think is, *where are the helicopters, the fire department, the ambulances? Where's the help?* It's been hours—this doesn't make any sense.

Unless...*did they already come?* They showed up already and thought I was dead. Or they didn't see me at all because I was too far off the road. They left me. No, surely that can't be—

When I gag again, I'm able to look away, and this time I don't hold back. My stomach empties itself of what little is left before I wipe my mouth.

Somehow it only now dawns on me that I have a cell phone. I reach into my pocket, but of course it's not there. I look back toward my truck, now engulfed by flames. Sweat prickles the back of my neck as the flames draw nearer. *What are the chances I'm actually going to find someone's cell—not broken, not melted?*

"Shit!"

I keep moving on to the next car and the next, but it's all the same. Car after car—no survivors. Everyone is dead. Phones either broken, not working, or gone. *How did no one else make it?*

When I find no one living, I do the only other thing I can think of—I scour for anything that might be useful, even besides cell phones. Who knows how long I'll be out here alone; food and water would be great. I wouldn't mind a flare gun or a radio, either. Anything to call for help or get me through until help gets here is going to be a lifesaver.

But somehow, there's nothing.

Somehow, the owners of the cars accessible to me were neat freaks who like to clean. There's nothing of value or use. No old fast food, no first-aid kits. I'm not MacGyver; I don't know how to turn a pen into a lightning rod or a napkin into a flamethrower.

A moment of helplessness overcomes me. I double over, nausea in my throat. My fists run through my hair as I fight back the urge to scream. *All those people...*they're gone.

"What the hell am I going to do now?"

I'm the only one left—at least on this part of the road. I don't have a clue what's going on. The only thing I do know is that the freeway is a raging inferno. There could be another explosion—or not. And I have nothing of use but my head and the clothes on my back.

Get the hell home, Ben.

I can't follow the road. The fire will probably spread into the forest—it might have already up ahead. I can't stay here either. It's too dark and too dangerous. Before I can stop myself by thinking of any more excuses, I move away from the freeway and into the forest.

SIX

Through the night, I stay close enough to the road to see the dim glow of fire on the horizon but far enough away to give me time to move if I have to. Crisp spring air and blood full of adrenaline have kept me awake. My mind won't stop running in circles, analyzing all the possible scenarios. *I'm an analyst*, I remind myself. It's what I do for a living.

The thought isn't comforting. Deep down, I know that this wasn't just some gas line explosion. It can't be explained away as *an accident*. There are too many variables indicating that there's foul play, and the worst part is knowing nothing. There's no one to ask, no news channel to watch. I'm completely on my own and not only that—with the freeway still burning, it could take me days to get home.

Days.

My mind reels. My wife and kids not knowing where I am, having no way to reach me, probably thinking I'm dead...*I can't leave things like this with Rachel.*

I have to get to them. Whatever it takes.

I n the morning, I take another look in the direction of the freeway to see the fire still raging. The flames hadn't reached me overnight, hadn't even come close. Lucky for me, they'd taken another direction. I want more than anything to go back to the road, but I know it would be a senseless waste of time.

Last night the fire was hot enough to melt the asphalt. I can only imagine what it would be like now. I'd spend time backtracking, only to have the heat prevent me from getting anywhere close enough to scavenge when instead I could be moving forward. *Get home. Get to Rachel and the kids.*

A feeling of being utterly alone fills me. No human beings anywhere, no animals, no phone, nothing but trees surrounding me, reaching into the smoke-filled sky. Have I ever been this disconnected? Not since I was a kid, I'm sure.

I can't follow the road, but it doesn't take GPS for me to know I can cut through the forest. The direction of home is the direction of home, whether I'm walking on asphalt or on dirt. *No big deal.*

Before I waste any more time, I set out—away from the freeway. The fire may be traveling in the other direction—for now, but the smoke isn't. Overhead, the sky is an ugly gray, thick with black smoke. The stench of burning is so strong I gag on it, and covering my nose and mouth with my jacket does nothing.

My movement through the forest is slow. I'm off balance at times, stumbling over my own feet along with broken branches and limbs. A few times I feel like I'm suffocating because I can't get enough clean air in my lungs with the exertion of winding my way through the trees.

My throat is coated with stale air, and no amount of trying to clear it works. I could kill for a drink of water, but the more I think about it, the worse the urge gets. I get to the point where even the dew on the leaves looks like a well of spring water.

As the day wears on, gradually my lungs find respite. I'm far enough away now that there's no longer a glow on the horizon. Forest animals are leery from my trespass through their domain, but I can sense their presence where I couldn't before.

I try not to stop because I know how long it's going to take, and every second counts. When I spoke to Rachel on the phone, I was still about sixty miles away. The freeway wasn't a straight shot to home. It wound around the forest, so now it's like taking a shortcut. I'm just not sure how much of one. Fifty miles on foot, on rough forest terrain, isn't what I'm used to, especially without water.

Hours pass, and my feet cry out for relief. My New Balance tennis shoes are a perfect comfort for a day in the office, not half a day hiking. My thighs, which haven't seen a gym in years, throb. My stomach, which also hasn't seen a gym in as long and has admittedly seen one too many beers lately, growls in hunger. I'm reminded of one of the most basic survival instincts—I need to eat.

As I stop walking, my aches seem to become worse, and a sudden, painful thirst almost brings me to my knees. "I'm never going to make it out here," I rasp. Looking around, it's achingly clear that I'm not going to be able to meet my most basic human needs. Food. Water. Shelter. How will I find them?

I won't be able to.

An image of my office comes to mind—of the five-gallon jugs of crystal-clear water stacked and waiting to be used, the communal fridge filled with lunches, the deli downstairs, the bathrooms with toilets and running water. I try not to choke. "It's fine. I'll be fine. It's just like camping for a few days. Backpacking without a backpack."

I lie to myself over and over, trying to keep from panicking. *Remember Rachel and the kids. They need you.* What would she say if she saw me here like this? On the verge of freaking out—of giving up just because I'm tired and hungry?

A chill comes over me, seeping down into my bones. It might be my lack of movement combined with the chilly air and now drizzle of rain, or it might be the look I imagine on my wife's face.

Break time's over, Ben.

I start moving again. And this time, I'm paying attention. A person can survive a couple of days without food and water, and that's all I need. Just a couple of days. I might feel like I'm about to die, but I'm not. I'm nowhere near it.

I almost cry when I see them. Blackberry bushes nearly as tall as I am. Thorny vines wind together, stretching and wrapping themselves around nearby trees and foliage and up into the leaves. I'd be drooling as I rush over, if I had any spare saliva.

When I reach them, I realize they're not in season. Instead of fresh, ripe berries to pick, all that's left are shriveled-up leftovers, picked over by deer and other wildlife and decayed by the elements.

As my anger and disappointment boil inside, I hear a faint noise. My heart leaps to my throat. Was that me or something else?

"Hello?" I rasp before clearing my throat and trying again. "Is someone there?"

No answer.

I listen, focusing as hard as I can. The noise didn't sound close...it could be someone out there, someone who survived the freeway just like me. Or it could be an animal.

"Are you hurt? Do you need help?" I try again. I take a few steps around the blackberry bushes to get a better view, and my breath catches.

There's a cabin.

SEVEN

The first thing I do is scour the place for food and water. It's a small hunting cabin, barely bigger than a closet. There's a bed and a roof, and that's about it, but it doesn't matter. I have shelter. I'm inside, out of the cold and the rain, and I don't have to worry about getting eaten in my sleep by whatever wild animal happens upon me.

There's a sink but no running water. Next to the bed is a small cabinet. My head spins as I open the doors and see a couple of canned goods along with a can opener. "Thank you," I whisper, reaching with a shaking hand toward the baked beans.

Please don't let this be a hallucination. I'm terrified that this is all in my head, even the cabin is a dream. I'm still out there, still wandering the forest, looking for food and shelter, still trying to get home but lost beyond imagination. Maybe I'm lying beneath a tree, slowly dying from dehydration and starvation. It'll take them weeks, maybe months or even years to find me.

Maybe they never will. Rachel and the kids—

My fingers grip the aluminum.

Canned beans have never tasted as good.

I t gets dark fast. There's no electricity and no way to
light the cabin, but I don't mind. What would I do
with them anyway? I'm not here on a vacation. My body
needs sleep and shelter from this place, nothing else.

I wish there was a way to thank the owner for saving
my life, because I'm sure that's what this place has done.
When this is over, I'll find a way to thank them.

With my hunger temporarily sated, I climb into the
small bed with no sheets or blankets, and within
moments I'm out.

Something nudges me. It takes me a moment to wake
—a cold hand slaps my face. I throw up my hands to
defend myself when something nudges me again—this
time a punch to my gut.

I roll off the bed, gasping for air.

"Time to wake up, buttercup," a deep voice says.

I look up to see the silhouette of a large man holding
a rifle. It's still the middle of the night and the headlamp
he's wearing nearly blinds me. "Who—" I start before he
turns the gun on me. "Wait a minute," I say, backpedal-
ing. "I'm sorry for trespassing. There was an accident—"

The man barks a laugh. "Get up, guy. We're going
outside."

My first thought—the only logical explanation in my
mind—is that this man is the owner of the cabin. It

explains why he's dressed in camouflage hunting gear, why he's carrying a gun, and why he'd wake me and want me out of his cabin. Something about his laugh though—something about his tone. It makes me pause.

"I'm not fucking with you," the man says, kicking at my leg with his boot.

Once I'm standing, he leads the way outside. I follow him into the crisp night air, no longer raining, wanting to ask him for water, for help. It's on the tip of my tongue. Then I see the others.

There are two other men outside waiting. Like the one who woke me, they're wearing headlamps that block me from seeing their features. What I can see—is that also like the first, they're armed.

"Let's go," one says, urging me forward.

"Look, I'm sorry—"

"Shut up. I said fucking move," the first says, pointing his gun at me again.

The third man, who hasn't yet spoken, approaches me with something in his hands. I try to shield my eyes from the light, but he grabs my wrist. I pull away from him, confusion turning to anger. Whoever the hell these guys are, something isn't right with them.

A rifle cocks. "I'd hold still if I was you," one of them says.

I freeze, brimming with anger and alarm. You don't just grab someone and hold them at gunpoint like this. This can't be because I was—am—on someone's property. *What the hell are they planning on doing?*

The third man reaches for my wrists again, and this time, he tightens a zip tie around me. The second man, who seems to have more of an authoritative air, takes the lead. He nudges me in the back with his gun, urging me to follow. He and the third man are behind me as we walk wordlessly back into the forest.

The entire time my mind is spinning. I could fight—but should I? And what then? Either they shoot me, and I die for nothing—or I get away, and I still don't know a damned thing. If they're hunters and this is their property or it was their cabin, then maybe they're just taking me to the police, which in that case, I want them to do. A sliver of hope shines through at that thought.

I need to tell someone about the freeway, about the fire, the people still in their cars—

It's clear these men don't want to listen to me, at least not yet. Maybe once they see I'm not a threat, they'll calm down.

After some time passes in silence, voices come from a distance. I look to the other's faces to judge their reactions, but none of them have any. They're not surprised at all.

It doesn't take long for me to learn why.

EIGHT

There's a small campfire and three men—two with their arms bound just like me. But unlike me, they're in bad shape. And when I say bad, I mean it looks like they've been through a one-sided boxing match. One's clothes are ripped and bloody, and the other's face looks like a peach that's been used as a punching bag.

A sinking feeling goes right to my gut. These men fought back. They didn't let anyone take them. They were made to go with or they were taken by force.

The man with torn clothes meets my gaze, and two things are now perfectly clear. These men with guns don't own the land or the cabin. And this is what I would look like too if I'd had the courage to stand up for myself instead of letting them lead me away.

How could I be so stupid?

"Sit over there," one of the armed men says, pushing my back with the gun's barrel. He urges me forward toward the other man who's bound and gagged, pushing me harder when I stumble.

Once I'm sitting, those who are armed walk away together. A couple of them swagger as if they just caught the biggest buck of their lives and seeing them this way, their confidence, their cockiness, while these other two men and I are sitting here bound and bleeding—it makes me sick.

Their voices come in hushed whispers, barely audible. I strain to hear, to make out anything at all, who they are, where they came from, what the hell they want with us.

The man with ripped and bloodied clothes mumbles something behind his gag.

The other, whose face is so swollen I'm not sure if he can even see, shakes his head. He's gagged too and doesn't try to speak.

Looking around first to make sure we're not being watched, I reach forward to pull the cloth from the bloodied man's mouth. The man's eyes widen. He shakes his head and pulls back from my open grasp.

"What is it?" I hiss.

He nods his head to the side while rolling his eyes in the same direction.

My gaze drifts down to the fire, where I see a knife. My heart jumps to my throat.

The man, who's too swollen to speak, shakes his head again. He releases a long low groan, almost like a plea to not do anything stupid.

Is that what got him looking the way he does? He tried to escape, and they beat him for it?

The man with bloodied clothes is still trying to get my attention, still trying to tell me something. I inch toward him, attempting to remain unnoticed by the group of armed men only feet away. Part of my brain tries to take in anything I can make out, but the other part is more concerned with the two beside me.

Unlike me, his arms are tied behind him instead of in front. He squirms, and I see there's something concealed in his jacket pocket. The more he moves, the more agitated the beaten man becomes. They're having some kind of argument with the noises they're making—the bloodied one growing angry, and the swollen one desperately pleading.

I feel torn between two sides, doing something stupid but at least *doing*, and *not* doing but also not getting my ass kicked or killed. I'm leaning more toward *not* doing, at least until I can get more information, but then the gun falls out of the pocket, landing on the ground with a soft thud.

The three of us stare at one another, eyes wide with terror. As one, we look toward the other group of men—they're all watching us, wearing amused expressions.

Fuck.

"What the hell do you think you're doing?" one of them calls to us.

They haven't seen the gun. They don't see it lying there. It's on our side of the fire, hidden behind the flames.

The man beside me, with ripped and bloodied clothing, lifts his eyebrows at me, giving me a barely susceptible nod. I know what he wants. He wants me to grab the pistol.

Of the three of us, I'm the only one whose hands are bound in front. I'm the only one who would stand a chance even trying to hold the thing, let alone shoot it.

It's suicide.

One pistol versus how many rifles? I may take a couple down with me, but for what? I'd still be going down.

I avert my eyes. I'm trying to be discreet but the man inches closer to me, still trying to get my attention, even with our captor's full attention on us. If I wasn't tied up, I'd slap the bastard for not getting the hint. *He's going to make them come over here if he keeps moving around like that!*

I want to move away from him, but I know I can't do that. I want to tell him to stop wiggling his fucking eyebrows around, and can't do that either. I want to tell the men with guns to do us all a favor and take a hike, but I sure as hell can't do that.

Sweat is starting to bead on my forehead, and I can tell the exact second the armed men realize something's wrong. The one who looks to be more the leader walks toward the campfire, coming around it to our side. He stares at each of the three of us, then his eyes land on the gun.

"What's that for?" He takes a step closer, leans down, and picks up the pistol. He points it at my forehead. "This yours?"

I can only shake my head *no.*

Laughter bursts out of him in a single gasp, like popping a balloon. "Just kidding, man, I know it's this fuck's." He turns to the man beside me. "I'm fucking *already* tired of your shit." Then he pulls the trigger.

I fall backward off the log, ears ringing, unable to hear the screaming of my own voice. Brain matter, blood, and bits of skull are plastered to my clothes, to me, my hair, are *inside* my mouth—I gag, vomit, gag again.

Behind me, the other bound man, who's already been beaten, is beaten again. One of our captors can't stop laughing, and another grabs me by my shirt, hauls me back over the log, and kicks me until I'm next to the fire.

The heat from the flames licks my face, cooking the gore onto me. I'm half in shock, unable to defend myself from the man beating me; all I can do is hold my bound hands up in an effort to protect my face. As I do, the rope starts to fray from the heat, and I realize this is my only chance.

Forget doing nothing. Forget not trying. If I'm going to wind up with *my* brains splattered over someone else anyway, at least let them say I wasn't a coward.

I leave my wrists as close to the heat as I can stand, gritting my teeth against both the onslaught of my captor's boot and the heat of the fire. My skin starts to blister and still I leave it until the rope is so tender I can feel it give when I try to separate my wrists.

I'm not able to see the other man being beaten, but I can hear him. His gag must've been removed because he cries out for mercy with every hit. "Please, please stop!" he screams. "I'll do anything! Stop!" His words are slurred between swollen gums and missing teeth.

Finally, when I think I'll catch fire before the rope, I break free. The knife, still hidden in the shadows of the rocks surrounding the fire, calls to me like a beacon of light.

With the last of my strength, I reach for it, then I bring it down on the bastard's leg the next time he comes for me. The man retreats, howling and cursing, bending down to hold his leg and inspect the damage.

The others are thrown off guard, but I don't stick around to see what they do. I force myself to stand. Then I run. I run for my life.

NINE

I run as fast as my legs will carry me, and then I push myself harder. My muscles cry out as I drive them to push my overweight body harder than I've ever done in my life. Panting, heaving, sweating as if I'm in a sauna, I run for my life.

The men call out for me to stop. Cursing and swearing, they yell at each other for letting me slip away. I keep going, even when there are gunshots, even when the bullets hit the trees around me.

As unfit and out of shape as I am, I haul ass. My son, who's the fastest kid I know, would beam with pride if he saw the way his dad was running now. There's something about running for your life that really puts a little pep in the step.

My chest tightens, but I don't slow, and no matter what they say, what they threaten, or what I hear them doing to the other man—I don't look back. I know that If I do, I'll either slow down or trip over myself. Either way, it'll be the end. They'll shoot me on the spot or make it so I can't get away again.

Thank god for adrenaline because if it wasn't for the naturally occurring chemical coursing through my veins, I would've been dead meat already. *I still might be.* As much as it's carrying me this far, I know there's no way I can keep it up. I can't outrun them.

There has to be a place to hide, a place to—I'm too focused on running, on not falling on my face or hitting a tree or having a goddamned heart attack. The land drops into a ravine ahead of me. I see it too late. I try to stop, to backpedal; it's too late. My arms flail and my jaw drops in a silent scream as I slide off the edge.

I tumble down the steep side of the hill in an almost vertical drop, my body spinning violently, thrashing against rocks, trees, and brush until I finally come to a stop at the bottom. Blood rushes in my ears as my head spins. When I force myself to get up, to keep going, my stomach lurches and I vomit bile.

"Come on, goddamnit!" I look toward the top of the ravine, desperate to see if the men are on their way down too, but it's impossible to tell.

They weren't that far behind!

I make it up on my feet, clenching my jaw to keep from yelling out. Even if they didn't try to beat the hell out of me, my trip down the side of the hill did the job enough for them. One of my legs feels like it's broken, maybe my arm or wrist too. It's hard to tell. My whole body aches. I'm bleeding badly, dizzy, and still nauseous.

To top it all off, I could probably take a shit, but I won't go there.

I hear water nearby—either a stream or river, and head for it without hesitation. The gentle gurgling against rocks is music to my ears and sends a sliver of hope surging through me. *The sound of the water might be enough to mask all the noise I make when I move.*

With effort, I make my way to it. The sight is beautiful, and at any other time, I might stop to appreciate the majesty. All I can think of now is wanting to dip down and drink my fill of the fresh, clear water, to clean the blood and gore off. My mouth aches for just a taste of it, enough to wet my tongue would be all it took, but I can't do it. Not yet.

There's no way to know how close those men are, if they're right behind me still and going to shoot me in the back any second, or up on the cliff's edge, wondering if I survived the fall. They could know a safe path down or still be trying to figure it out. Either way, my injuries have also slowed me down to barely a crawling pace, and if I stop, if I bend to reach for the water—I won't get back up. Not today. So, I keep moving.

When I pass a suitable branch, I take it and lean on it like a crutch to ease some of the pain in my leg. I find another smaller one to bite on, to keep from screaming when I tie part of my shirt around it to stop the bleeding. There's nothing I can do for my arm or other injuries, so I tuck it in close to my chest, cradling it as best I can.

Walking on my leg is agony. Blood oozes around my makeshift bandage as I continue forward, the coppery smell filling my senses. *This is bad. This is really, really bad.*

I know I need to stop the bleeding. Everything I've

ever heard or learned about injuries tells me this, but every instinct to my core tells me to keep going. *I'm moving too slow to stop. I can't stop yet.*

I allow my body to move on autopilot, following the water through the forest as it eventually turns into a river. There are times I almost pass out from the pain, but somehow, I manage to maintain consciousness.

My body needs rest, needs help. It cries out for it, begging me with every step I take, and I ignore it the same way I might've ignored my kids whining for a treat they didn't deserve. How long has it been since I've seen them? Twenty-four hours now? Looking at the sky, at the sun now looming behind the clouds, it's hard to tell what time of day it is. Definitely not the middle of the night anymore.

Why did this have to happen? I was just trying to get home from work. I'd give anything to see my family now, to see my damned bed—

I shake my head, forcing the thoughts to go. I don't need to pity myself. I need to get through this. I need to survive whoever the hell those people are. The river will take me to a city or a town. That's what rivers do. It's just a matter of time.

And just as I start to believe it, to allow myself to hope, I come around a bend to see a small raft pulled to the shore. My eyes widen at the sight of it. I look around, wondering who else could be here. It could belong to those men, and if so, they'll be coming for it.

It looks like it's been here a while though...how long have they been here?

Movement comes behind me. I spin and scan the trees on pins and needles. *It's them! It has to be them!*

Unintelligible voices, not yelling, but that tone—they're close enough now for me to hear, and that's too close for my taste.

Without another thought, I push the raft into the water and climb inside.

TEN

There's a single oar inside the raft, but I'm far too weak to attempt using it. Instead of trying to fight the current, I allow it to carry me along as I duck low out of sight. *Come on, come on,* I silently urge the water to pick up the pace as I peer over the edge to watch the tree line, waiting for someone to step through at any moment.

When I'm carried along, around another bend and out of sight, I finally release a breath. Some of the tension eases from my muscles, and I allow myself a moment to relax while I bend down to drink and clean myself.

The gentle rocking of the current is soothing, so soothing that before long, I'm growing drowsy. My eyes grow heavy, and I catch myself drifting more than once.

"Wake up!" The sound of my own voice jostles me back to the present. I reach a hand into the water and splash myself, the ice-cold river waking me back up.

"It's not safe enough to sleep. Not yet," Rachel's voice says in my mind.

Yeah, you can say that again.

Where there's water, there's civilization, I remind myself over and over, a sense of foreboding growing inside with every turn of the river. I'm being carried deeper into the forest, not away from it, and I'm not sure if I'm getting myself into a worse situation rather than a better one.

The water is getting rougher, the current choppier. The raft begins to sway harder, tossing me around to the point I have no choice but to pick up the oar. Without it, I'll tip and probably drown. I hang on to the wooden handle for dear life, struggling against the pain in my body to keep the small boat afloat.

Soon, I hear a sound that turns my blood to ice. My eyes nearly bulge out of my head when I realize what it is. *No, no, no! This is not happening to me!* Ahead, the river isn't taking me to civilization. There's a drop-off. It's taking me to a waterfall.

Panic takes over, giving me more strength than I've ever had. I row for my life, trying to get to the shore before it's too late. I get close to a large boulder, try to wedge the raft between it and the shore, and try to get myself leverage, but it's no use. I think about diving in and swimming for it, but I realize that's suicide.

I keep rowing, screaming with the effort. I get close enough to some large overhanging branches, knowing I'll only have a split second to grab on. I have to stop rowing to reach for them, and once I do, if I miss and catch air instead, I might not have another chance.

This is it.

I drop the oar and stretch.

My fingers touch nothing. An image flashes before

my eyes, my body falling, crashing below the water, smashing into shallow rocks, crushed beneath thousands of pounds of pressure from the falls.

I reach again.

Then my fingers brush the edge of the branch. I claw at it, and once I have it in my grip, I'm glued on. I pull myself and the raft in, using the rest of my depleted reserves to get to the shoreline. There are too many rocks in the way for the raft. Unwilling to let go of the branch for anything—it's the only thing keeping me alive—I pull myself up off the raft. Half swimming, half pulling, I finally heave myself onto the shore.

I watch the raft float away. Within seconds it falls into oblivion.

The ground is mostly level when I stand, *thank god.* It's hard enough to stand and walk, I can only imagine what I'd look like trying to hobble down the side of another hill. My bones ache with exhaustion, my eyes honing in on every log that looks like a good place to sit. *Not yet, goddammit*, I remind myself. *They could still be after me. I have to go a little farther.*

I settle for using a large branch as a new makeshift crutch to support some weight as I walk since the last one floated away with the raft. It's also my only means of defense if I do run into those men again. *Let's hope it doesn't come to that.*

The day is long and painful. After hours of trying to navigate through a forest, where I now have no idea—not even a clue—of where I am, I'm growing clumsy from exhaustion. I've stumbled countless times, narrowly missing falling on my ass and tearing open my injuries, or worse. The bleeding has slowed, but the bandage is soaked through, and the pain—I've felt nothing like it.

I can imagine my wife telling me, "*get to a hospital,*" or "*don't put weight on that leg.*" She'd fuss over it and baby me until I could get to a doctor. It's been less than forty-eight hours and I'm falling apart without her.

I close my eyes, willing myself to get through this when the branch I'm leaning on hits a rock. It jerks to the side, and I'm too off-balance to catch myself. I cry out as I fall forward, landing on my bad leg.

It takes me a few minutes to recover enough to look around from this new point of view, and when I do, I realize there's another cliff. This time, though, the opening is wide open and clear, so gritting my teeth against the pain, I make my way toward it.

"Holy cow."

From this view, I can see where the river drops off to the waterfall in the distance. I gulp at the sight of the falls, trying not to tremble at what else I see. On the horizon, there are buildings. A town, visible, right there, waiting for me. I'm not lost anymore, not going to die out here alone. All I have to do is keep hanging on.

ELEVEN

As I navigate the forest, the closer I get to the town, the more dread grows in the pit of my stomach. There's something wrong with the forest. There are too many fallen limbs, and not enough wildlife. *Something has been through here.*

I think about the men who found me, who took me and probably would've killed me or done only God knows what else. Did they come through here too? They were on foot as far as I could tell, but that doesn't mean they didn't have a vehicle of some kind accessible to them.

Another night comes, cold and alone, this time without shelter, and even if I were able to start a fire, I'd be too terrified of attracting attention. Instead, I huddle up next to the trunk of a tree, shivering against myself. *At least the cold helps numb the hurt.*

When I dare look beneath the bloody bandage around my leg, it's hard not to grimace. "Don't get infected," I beg, knowing it may already be too late. The skin is inflamed and swollen, and though not actively bleeding, it oozes when I move. I toss the bandage, ripping off another piece of my clothing to wrap around.

"I need to find a hospital. I need to get to that town."

I'm met with pure silence. No hooting owls, no scurrying critters, nothing.

Overhead, the starless sky is smoke filled, and so dark I can barely see. I close my eyes and wait for morning.

I wake in the dark to the sound of a throat clearing. Standing in front of me is the other man who was tied up by the fire—the one whose face was so swollen I thought he probably couldn't see. I thought for sure they killed him too, but he's...here.

Without the gag in his mouth, I'm able to get a somewhat better image of him, but he still looks worse than before. *How did he get here? How did he find me?*

"They didn't kill you," I say when I finally find words.

"You saved my life," he says.

I sit up a little straighter at that. "How can you say that? I ran. I left you at their mercy."

His bruised cheeks lift into something of a lopsided smile. "What you did was distract the hell out of them. They were so worried about getting you back, they forgot all about kicking my ass, and I was able to slip away too." He shrugs. "Without the distraction, I probably would be dead."

"How the hell did you make it this far? Look at you—you look about at death's door. How'd you find me?"

The man comes forward, taking a seat on the ground beside me. "I saw you get on the raft. I would've called to you, but I didn't want to draw their attention. So, I knew you were on the river, and I followed."

His words make sense. Everything adds up. But it's a little too good, almost like a script that's been thought out. For some reason, I just can't put my finger on, it doesn't add up the way it should. And if he saw me—did they see me too?

This man was being beaten to a bloody pulp when I got away. I don't know how he can move at all, let alone walk this far—even I didn't have to do that. And...he would've had to drop off the ravine like I did...or know that I was down there, and the others were *right* on my ass.

I chew on my bottom lip, staring at him while at the same time trying to listen for others. There's not much I can say. I'm not going to call the man a liar. He's basically in the same boat as me; why would he need to lie?

He must sense my unease because he finally breaks the silence. "Your leg looks bad. I thought for sure I'd never catch up to you, but seeing that thing explains a lot."

He's right. Chill out already, Ben.

"It's bad, but I can walk. I need to get some antibiotics...you wouldn't happen to have any of those, would you?"

The man huffs. "No, but wouldn't mind a round myself." He works his jaw. "What's your name? I guess I should know who saved my sorry ass. I'm Jack."

I take Jack's offered hand. "Ben."

"You know where we're going, Ben?"

I hesitate before pointing. "There's a town that way. I'm turned around, but I saw it with my own eyes from up the hill."

Jack nods. "I'm game. We need to keep moving anyway. Those bastards will be hunting us like dogs."

"Jack?"

"Yeah?"

"Who exactly are those men?"

"I..." He opens his mouth, closes it, and opens it again. "I don't know," he finally admits. He shakes his head. "So much happened so fast. There was an explosion on the freeway that killed hundreds—"

"I was there!"

"Jesus."

"I blacked out, and I was trapped and then moving through the forest, just trying to get home when those assholes found me. I don't know a goddamn thing that's happening."

"Well, after the explosion, there was another and another. Bombs were planted all over the main roads, emergency services in chaos. People ran. And...there were people like them." He points back toward the forest, indicating our captors. "Who were ready to...*catch* them."

Jack looks at me, tears pooling in his eyes. "They're holding people hostage, Ben. I don't know what they're doing with them. I don't know where they're going. But it sure as shit can't be good. I tried to run, so did Steve. You saw what they did to him in the end, what they did to me —to you."

Steve must've been the man with the ripped clothes— my eyes drift to my shirt, where his brain matter is still caked on. There's no question about the captors anymore.

They're not here to help, not here to guide people to safety. They're nothing but killers.

I close my eyes, thinking of Rachel and the kids. "Where did you say the explosions were happening?"

"All over hell and back. Along the major highways and main roads mostly. That was until they got me. I don't think they touched the big city. They were targeting small towns, easier prey."

All this happened from the time the road exploded to last night? They had to have planned for months or years to organize this quickly.

"Welldeer? Did you hear anything about—"

"I'm sorry," Jack says. And from the look on his face, I can tell. My wife and kids are not safe.

"People stayed home, though, right? I mean, there would be no reason to leave, right?" I work my way up off the ground, trying to convince myself that Rachel wouldn't leave without me. If the roads were being blown up, she would stay home, where it was safe. *Until someone knocks down the door—*

"Fuck!" I yell, answering myself.

Jack doesn't say a word. He doesn't have to.

It's impossible to really sleep or to get comfortable, but the rest is good. When dawn comes, I'm so cold I can feel it in my bones. It's a different kind of ache, one that makes me fear hypothermia. When I struggle back to my feet, I notice frost covering part of the forest floor.

Time to get going.

Grabbing my stick to lean on, Jack and I move toward the town.

As we draw nearer, something becomes painfully obvious. Burned trees and debris cover an area of forest that's almost completely destroyed. The fire is out, but the ground is still warm from the fire that swept through. I didn't notice smoke before...I wonder how long ago the fire happened.

Just on the outskirts of the town, buildings are visible through gaps in the burned trees. *No. Please*—my mind lurches in a dark direction, a direction that sounds crazy even to myself. Desperation comes over me, more than even when I was trapped inside my truck on a burning freeway. One thought consumes me—*I have to see.*

Terror beats pain.

I'm numb as I rush forward, hobbling with my stick toward the edge of town, Jack on my heels. My injuries are gone, along with my hunger and thirst, as I see the burned town of East Elk before my eyes.

TWELVE

This can't be happening. I shake my head, trying to clear the vision before my eyes. I even pinch myself, but nothing changes my view of the desolate streets, void of life. Everyone is—gone. Buildings are burning or already turned to ash, cars are wrecked, doors left open. The place is—abandoned. *What the hell happened here?*

I feel like I've been in a coma for years, instead of walking through a forest for three days. This is *insane*. I hobble forward, taking everything in while leaning on my branch. "I know this town," I say

"East Elk," Jack says, reading a sign. "We're less than twenty miles from Welldeer."

As ashamed as I am to admit it—relief is my first emotion because it's not home that this happened to. The feeling is immediately followed by guilt and anger. It might not be my home, but this town is still someone else's.

"How the hell could this happen? Where is the help? Where the fuck are the people?" I breathe. Am I that slow? I missed help not only on the freeway, but here, too?

"I tried to tell you," Jack says with a look.

Nothing about this makes any sense. There's not another soul in sight, and I'm pretty sure that's *not* how these things go. There should be investigators, at the very least... shouldn't there? Jack has to be wrong about something.

I'm so wrapped up in my confusion I find myself wandering off the main road onto a side street, where it becomes clear the fire was isolated. There's damage to some homes in this part of town, but no more evidence of fire. We stop at the front of an open door. The house's roof looks partially caved in; the front windows shattered. It looks dangerous. *There might be food inside.*

"Hello?" I call out, hoping I'm wrong, that there really are people around and everyone is just safe in their homes.

I wait a few moments. No answer comes. Jack tries, "Hey, anyone home?"

Still no response, so we step inside.

Debris and glass cover the entry and living room. It's a struggle with my leg, but eventually I make it past to the kitchen, where my mouth waters at the sight of the kitchen sink. Without thinking, my body moves on autopilot. Turning the faucet on, I lean over and take in as much liquid gold as I'm able. I drink and drink until my belly is full, and my throat no longer feels like sand-paper. Then I move toward the cabinets to search for food.

It's amazing what a little nourishment will do. Twenty minutes ago, I was dead on my feet, and now with a belly full of food and water, I feel like I can keep going for hours. Now that I can think a little more clearly, a to-do list races through my mind, pulling me in twenty different directions at once.

We need to get a car—it's the fastest, easiest way to get home, especially with my leg. I should get extra food too, just in case. We need to find a radio, see if there's an emergency broadcast—the car will have one most likely. We need to get help. I need to figure out what the hell—

A movement from the back of the house pulls me from my thoughts.

"What was that?" Jack and I share a look before each turning toward the hallway.

"Hello?" I call.

The movement stops.

I wait, then try again. "Please, is someone there? We need to know what's going on."

Silence.

I start for what I assume are the bedrooms, terrified of what—and who—I might find. *What if it's those men again? Ready to capture us...* My mind cries out.

It's not them. If it was, they wouldn't be so shy.

Okay, what if it's not them but someone like them? Maybe an angry homeowner with a gun, ready to blow your head clean off your shoulders?

I pause in the hallway, listening. "Please, if anyone's there, I don't mean any harm. I was in an accident on the freeway. We just got here, and we don't know what's happening."

Silence, still.

I keep moving. Inside one of the bedrooms, a pair of legs caked in dried blood and bruises peek out from beneath rubble from the collapsed roof. My stomach heaves at the sight, at the same time, my mind cries out, *run! Get the hell out of here, Ben!*

I know I can't run though. This person needs my help. "Hey, I'm here. Don't move. Let me see what I can do," I say to the legs. From their twisted angle, it's hard to see which way the person's head lays.

"We need to go in there, Jack." I turn to him for help.

He shakes his head, taking a step back to distance himself. "Look at them, Ben. They're dead."

"We need to make sure. We can't just leave them."

He takes another step away, holding up his hands as if to shield himself. The fear is radiating off him in waves. "I'm not going in there," he says.

If I had to go through what he did, I'd probably be the same, I tell myself. I take another peek inside the room and realize that Jack is probably right. *It doesn't matter. I still have to make sure. Besides—* "We heard something."

Jack scoffs. "That could've been anything."

"Or it could've been someone trying to get out from under the fallen roof."

Jack slinks farther down the hallway. "I'm not going to stop you from going in—even though I should—but don't think I'm coming to help if something goes south."

"What do you mean, you should stop me?" My irritation is unmistakable.

"I mean," Jack says, exasperated. "We should get moving. Those men are looking for people, Ben. Who knows how long it will take them to circle around to us."

How do we really know that? How do we know what happened in this town has anything to do with those people in the forest? It could be totally different people, unrelated, and we're *assuming* they're still after us. "You're right. I'll be quick," I say. Better to do it myself than continue to stand here and argue with him.

Jack says, "I'll take a look at the other rooms."

Taking a few steps into the room, I take in the details—the wooden beams, the sheetrock, the insulation, the broken furniture. *This person is already dead, just like Jack said.* They were lying on the bed when the roof caved. The legs haven't moved, toes haven't even twitched.

"Can you hear me?"

Nothing.

"Move so I know you're with me. Wiggle or something —anything—"

Nothing.

*They might be paralyzed, unable to move. I can't just leave them...*I look around for anything that might help me get through the debris. I still have my stick but—*Jesus, am I really going to do this?*

I shake my head at myself before starting to climb. I slip, move, fall through some cracks, move some more. I fight to get through, ripping open my already damaged leg in the process. I know it's stupid. I know it. But I won't be able to look my kids in their eyes if I leave without making sure.

Finally, feeling like I'm half dead myself, I reach the legs. They're cold. Whoever this was, they're long gone.

J ack shuffles through one of the bedrooms down the hall while I move to the last. Moving past the bed, I pull out the nightstand drawers to shuffle through the contents. Nothing greets me but some reading glasses and an old novel.

Continuing my search, I move on to the dresser. *Come on, give me something! A phone or some pain pills, maybe...* Drawer after drawer is filled with nothing but useless clothes. Underwear, T-shirts, socks, something rubbery that makes me jump back—*I don't want to know what the hell I just touched*—then my fingers feel cold, hard steel.

The handgun is small, one of those conceal carry kind, perfect for the glovebox or a woman's purse. Next to it is a clip filled with bullets. I slip the clip in the pistol and pocket it just as Jack calls to me, "Any luck in there?"

"Nothing," I call back.

He comes to the doorway, eying me warily.

He didn't see, I tell myself, willing my sweat glands to take it easy. I'm a nervous sweater, always have been.

Jack holds up a cell phone. "The screen is cracked, but it works."

My heart leaps to my throat. "Did you—"

"The towers are down, or the lines are congested. Whatever's going on, it doesn't matter if the phone works because calls aren't getting through."

"We'll keep trying."

Jack nods his agreement. "Come on, there's some cars outside we can look through."

Wrecked, locked, or empty. Jack and I spend precious time looking through cars only to come up empty-handed. This part of town may still be intact, but we're having a hell of a time finding anything else useful.

"There's nothing here," I say. "I saw a sign for an urgent care center back the other way. We should get going." Both of us are barely able to move. We were lucky enough to fill our bellies. Now we need to get medicine before infection sets in.

"Wait a minute." Jack points up the street. "There's a semi. It might have a radio."

We make our way toward it, me still using my branch for support and Jack seeming to have no issues with walking other than a slight limp. No matter what he says, I can tell he has problems seeing by the way he tilts his head back at an odd angle to get a better view. He makes it to the tipped truck, bending down to climb inside before I catch up.

"You see anything?" I call.

"There's a CB. Hang on."

I'm glad he knows what he's doing because I sure wouldn't. Minutes pass as I listen to Jack shuffling through the cab and saying things I can't quite make out on the radio. I look up at the sky with a sinking feeling.

We're going to have to spend the night here. Whether that's a good idea or a bad one, only time can tell—either way, I think it's probably better than another night in the forest. *I hope.*

Jack crawls back out from the semi. He frowns at me. "Nothing but static."

"You want to try the phone again?"

"Already did. Still nothing."

I flatten my lips as anger flares. "Alright. Listen, I don't want to be a dick, but you mind if I try?" I hold out my hand, and to my surprise, Jack hands the phone over without question.

"Be my guest," he says.

I dial 9-1-1, and just like Jack said before, the call won't go through. I clear the screen and this time, try my wife's phone. This time, there's a pause before I hear ringing. "Holy shit," I whisper.

"What?" Jack stares at me with bated breath.

And just like that—the call ends. Two quick beeps. I look at the screen. *Call failed*, stares at me before *Low battery* flashes with a red battery icon. Then the screen goes black.

"No!" I cry, my fingers pressing every button I can think of. I try to restart the thing, try to dial 9-1-1 again, press the power button five times, try the volume—anything to get it to come back to life. From the corner of my eye, Jack takes a step back. I spin on him. "You didn't tell me it had a low battery!"

"I didn't know!"

"If you used the thing, you had to know, Jack. What the hell? I could've waited until we were farther away, had a better signal, anything!"

Jack holds up his hands. "Okay, look, I'm sorry. I didn't want you to lose hope, is all. I wanted us to have something to hold on to. If you knew it was going to die—I just didn't want you to lose your shit, like you're clearly doing."

"You had no right to hide it from me."

Jack gives me a pointed look.

My face heats under his scrutiny, the handgun heavy in my pocket. *A gun is different*, I tell myself. If I can't trust the man with a phone, how the hell am I going to trust him with a gun?

"If we're done here, we better keep moving. It'll be dark soon," Jack says.

Why hasn't he called me out about the gun? He knows I'm hiding it—or maybe not it, but *something*, and yet he hasn't said a word. Whatever the reason, I'm glad. One less confrontation for now.

I hand the dead phone back to him. He can keep it or throw it or do whatever the hell he wants with the useless thing. I don't care anymore. "Lead the way," I say.

THIRTEEN

With every step we take through this town, there's a nagging at the back of my mind that won't go away. *Where the hell is everyone?* A few times, as I look through store windows, I could swear I see people hunched over in hiding. I want to call to them, to ask them what happened and where everyone else is—to ask why they're hiding, *who* they're hiding from.

Isn't it obvious though? They're hiding from whoever or whatever destroyed the roads and half the buildings. Whether Jack is right that our captors had anything to do with it remains to be unseen, but these people are probably looking at Jack and me like we're suicidal idiots for walking down the middle of the road the way we are.

"Do you know where we're going?" I ask Jack, about five or six feet in front of me.

He points ahead. "I think it's just past that shopping center."

Within a few minutes, we're staring at the outside of

an urgent care building that looks like it's been burned to a crisp. "Well, that's a no-go," Jack says.

"We might be able to find something inside still."

"You're joking, right?" He narrows his eyes at me. "The place went up in smoke. Look at it!"

"Look at the second floor. It doesn't look like it's been touched. We could try—"

"And how the hell do you plan to get *up* there?"

I grind my teeth, once again, holding back from lashing out at this guy. He's so afraid to do anything, to *try* anything. Maybe because of the men who beat the hell out of him, and maybe not. Either way, I'm getting tired of being told we can't do it without even giving it a goddamn shot.

"Stay here if you want to. I'm going to walk around the back and have a look." I set off around the other side of the building without waiting.

Lord, I miss my wife. The thought is sudden and overwhelming, almost bringing me to my knees. We don't have a perfect marriage—who does? We argue almost daily sometimes, but Rachel is a problem solver. She would figure something out and put Jack in his place while she was at it. She doesn't understand the word *can't.*

Around the back, part of the building is crumbling, and the sight only makes me glad that Jack didn't follow. I'm not in the mood to hear about how *unsafe* it looks. If I don't get some antibiotics, my leg is toast. Going into the rubble is worth the risk.

I latch on to the fire escape and climb.

Reaching the second floor in one piece, I start down the hall with a smug smile. *I can't wait to show Jack what I find.* I take two steps and the floor drops out from under me. My foot punches through the burned floor, the ground caving beneath me. I yell out, reaching to grab anything to hold on to. As I do, I'm falling, my good leg dangling in mid-air as the weight of my body drags itself down.

Calloused fingers grasp my outstretched hand, and I hang on for dear life as Jack pulls me back up. We stare at each other for a moment, both panting. "I told you it's not—"

Jack is cut off mid-sentence as the entire floor caves. Jack and I both fall, along with the floor and everything else around us. My breath is gone, my lungs frozen, unable to inhale a breath to scream. In slow motion, I watch Jack land, watch his body collide with the burned rubble of the first floor, then I watch as the entire second floor smashes his body into dust.

I wake up in the dark, barely able to breathe. There's someone else here. My first thought is of Jack, hope surging forward. *He made it! He's alive!* But I remember the way he landed, the way his body caved in on itself and the sickening crunch...no, there's no way Jack made it. There's someone else here.

I lie as still as I can, attempting to surface from the guilt. *What the hell was I thinking?* I will my heart rate and breathing to slow so I can listen.

There's one—no, two people, rummaging around. Their whispers are quiet. I want to ease myself closer, but there's no way to do so without making noise. I'm still half buried in the contents of the second floor.

"Are we still going to the survivor's camp?" one says.

"Soon. We need to make sure it's safe," the other replies.

"They'll have food. I'm starving, Molly."

"I know. But how do you know they're not the ones who did all this in the first place?"

"Who cares? If they have food and shelter—"

"*Who cares?* Trish, how the hell can you say that to me?"

"I just meant—"

"I don't give a shit what you meant." She sighs. "Look, we'll go over to Stillwater. The houses around there are probably empty and loaded."

I take my chance when their voices move away. I shift, willing my body to get up, groaning at the pain, not only from my injuries from being beaten and my fall down the ravine, but now from falling from the second floor of a building. I have to have so many broken bones right now, and I'll be lucky if I don't have internal bleeding or worse.

My mind reels at the conversation I overheard, and I use it as a point of focus while I push past the agony of getting to my feet. *A survivor's camp.* With food and shelter... they want people to go to this camp. Why? They think there will be another attack. It gives an explanation of sorts as to why the town is so empty but still doesn't explain where all the other help is.

I'm on my feet now, a little unsteady, but at least I'm up. I make my way toward the voices I heard moments ago, near blind in the dark. I keep tripping and lurching forward, and all I can think is *I cannot afford to fall again. Who knows what'll break this time?*

"Hello? Can I get some help?" I call out to the others, deciding to take my chances. I wait for a response, but it's suddenly so quiet I can hear my heart in my ears. Pulse pounding, I try again, a little louder. "Please, I know you're there." My voice comes out dry and raspy, my throat burning.

Whoever is or was here isn't going to answer. With no other choice, I stumble forward again, holding my hands out for balance. The going is slow, unsteady, and painful, but eventually I make it to something solid.

The longer I'm here, the more my eyes adjust to the dark, and I realize it's not the entire first floor that was burned like we originally thought. Movement comes from behind me again. A shifting in the rubble, not quite like the rummaging I heard moments ago.

"Whoever's there, I'm not going to hurt you. I would appreciate a little help," I call.

"Ben?" a croaking, rasping voice coughs.

I freeze. *There's no way he survived that fall—*

"Are you—" More coughing.

"Holy shit, Jack, is that you?"

"Help."

I move through broken pieces of the second floor, piled with burned and busted medical equipment, struggling to find him, until I see his head. "I'm here," he says.

"I see you, Jack. I'm coming."

When I'm close enough, Jack holds a gun outstretched, hands trembling. "You weren't the only one with a little secret. I know you found a gun in that house, Ben. Well, so did I."

I pause, trying to reach for the gun in my pocket—but it's gone. *What the hell is he planning?* "Jack..."

"I'm not going to die here."

I shake my head. "Of course you're not. Let me help you."

"This is all your—" More coughing and hacking. "Your fault," he finishes.

"Jack, I'm so sorry this happened." I blink, torn between looking away from the sight of his mangled body and forcing myself to meet his gaze.

The crunching I thought I heard—thought I *saw*, wasn't wrong. Jack's body is flattened beneath a section of the second floor. What little of him sticks out from beneath is a twisted, purple, bloody mess. I'm not sure if he freed his face somehow or if it was spared by blind luck.

He's right. This is my fault. If I hadn't insisted on going into a half-burned-down building, he wouldn't be lying on the floor dying.

"You're going to get me the hell out of this," Jack says.

"You don't have to hold me at gunpoint. I'll help you."

"I'm just done being pushed around. I know you're going to leave me here just like before."

"No, I'm not going to leave you. You saved my life, Jack. And you said that I saved yours by leaving. You thanked me, remember?"

"That's bullshit, and you know it."

I try to remain as calm as possible as Jack coughs again, this time blood spraying from his mouth. Even if I can figure out a way to get him out from under all the wreckage, he's not going to make it. Does he realize that?

Gradually, I make my way closer to him, picking at

smaller pieces of debris. His cough grows into a deep rattling that sounds like death. "Hurry," he says between breaths.

"Jack, I'm not in great shape myself."

"I don't give a shit what shape you're in!" he cries, cocking the gun and waving it around wildly. "I'm so sick—"

The sound of a gun firing makes me flinch and cover my head in an automatic reaction. When I realize I'm not dead, I look back to Jack—whose head is now gone.

No.

"Hey, are you okay?" a voice calls.

I turn to see two figures standing with a shotgun poised. Jack didn't kill himself. Whoever these people are, they killed him.

FOURTEEN

"What the hell did you do!" I yell, holding my hands out to steady myself.

The one holding the gun lowers it. The other comes toward me. "We mean no harm," she says.

"No harm? You just blew his fucking head off!"

"He had a gun! He was going to shoot you."

"He was just scared."

The woman stands in front of me. "I'm sorry if we were wrong. We made a split-second call, thinking we were saving your life. We were trying to help." She looks me up and down, grimacing. "*Do* you need help?"

They just killed Jack.

He was going to die anyway...

But they shot him in cold blood. Are they right? He was going to kill me. Maybe.

"Yes, I need help," I say. "Don't kill me too in the meantime, okay?"

Her friend comes toward me, and together they help

get me away from Jack. "I'm Molly," the one without the gun says. She points to her friend. "This is Trish."

"Ben," I reply between clenched teeth, trying not to scream from the agony of walking on my broken body. "I think my adrenaline is wearing down here pretty quick. Have either of you found any painkillers?"

"Just hang tight," Molly says.

A hallway stands, nearly untouched by flame, almost in perfect condition as much as I can tell. I almost cry with relief when we turn the corner and come to an open doorway. It's an exam room.

The three of us take a step inside, Molly and Trish helping me up on the exam table while they move to a storage cabinet. "Wish there was light," Trish mumbles under her breath.

"You're in luck, Ben," Molly smiles back at me. "We've got pain pills."

I start to get up off the table but fall, unable to stop from screaming as I land, yet again, on my injuries. Black creeps into the corners of my vision as Molly and Trish rush to help.

"You idiot, what were you thinking?" Trish says, slipping her arm beneath my back.

Fading fast, about to lose consciousness, I blink, willing my body to maintain control. *Get back up.* Slowly, I work my way back up off the floor. As I rise, I get a good look at the cabinet. The shelves are filled with boxes and bottles and pouches.

"You could've waited two more seconds." Molly reprimands.

My heart lurches as she approaches with antiseptic wipes in hand. *Finally, something goes right!* I dare to smile as she hands over a small pack of painkillers—not prescription strength, but maybe enough to do something.

"Thank you."

"You're welcome. Don't do anything stupid again, okay?"

I nod. *Don't plan on it.*

As I clean and re-wrap my injuries with the fresh supplies, I still don't have a good picture of myself, but it doesn't matter. The aching, the torment, is enough to tell me I'm in trouble. Falling from the second floor may not have killed me, but it took its toll.

"You two won't leave me, will you?" I hate how I sound, but I also don't care. It's so good to have help, to not be alone when I really need it. And I'll admit it—help is exactly what I need right now, if only for a few hours.

"We'll be right here on the floor," Trish says.

"Thank you for saving me," I say, popping the pain pills, lying back, and letting the darkness take me.

FIFTEEN

Rays of sunlight wake me, along with so much pain. When I finally get a look at my injuries, I wish I hadn't. The sight alone makes me sick.

For a moment, I can't remember how I wound up in this room until Molly's voice from the floor makes me jump out of my own skin.

"How do you feel?" she asks, chuckling when she sees me jump.

"I feel like I got hit by a big rig," I answer.

"You look like it too." She smiles a little. "Sorry, didn't mean to scare you."

She and Trish help me up off the exam chair. Once I'm standing, I see the cabinet that was so forthcoming last night, and now that it's daylight, I can see what I'm doing when I grab a few more handfuls of the painkillers and shove them in my pockets for later. There's a locked drawer I pry open, and inside, antibiotics. This time my eyes do water, and I don't bother to wipe them.

"You didn't see this last night?"

"It was kind of dark," Trish says with a shrug.

I glare at her as they each move to a side and help me back into the hallway, but it's not like I can really complain, is it? At least I found them now.

Down the hall, there's another supply closet with medical equipment and—a set of crutches. "Tell me I'm not dreaming," I say, staring as Molly hands them over.

"If you are, I am too." She smiles.

"Now all we need is food and water. I can't believe how lucky I've been in this place."

"Uh, you forgot about your friend pretty quick," Trish says.

Jack.

Well, I *have* been lucky—I didn't get crushed the way he did. I know that's dark, but it's also true, and add in the medicine, crutches, and the fact that this place wasn't burned to a crisp like we believed. If I would've listened to Jack, would've kept going instead of trying the second floor...*he'd be alive.*

I sober. Yeah. He'd be alive, and I'd maybe not be so broken. I take one of the crutches and keep moving.

There's nothing left for me in this town. I found as much medicine as I probably will. I'm not prepared to spend any more time looking for more or risk running into my captors again if they are indeed still looking for me.

I need to get home. To my wife and my kids. I need to

make sure they're okay, to reassure them that *I'm* okay, I'm not dead, I'm still kicking.

No more wasting time.

There's only one more thing I need before I leave. My stomach growls in protest as we make our way back down the main road. Food. Another fill-up, then I'm out of this ghost town.

"Where are you two headed?" I ask, my own decision made. And, now that I have time to think about it, I add, "And what were you doing at the urgent care?"

They share a look before Molly answers. "There's a neighborhood up the road with some nice homes. They'll have full pantries, and we all need food."

"You know, I've been thinking about that. Jack and I went into a house before...but why don't we try a grocery store or something, instead of someone's home?"

"We could...but there's a lot of people taking refuge there. That's the first place we actually tried, and let's just say they're not very welcoming."

"So people in a home would be?" That's hard to believe. I think Jack and I got a little lucky the first go around...

"I'd rather face one homeowner with a gun than a whole store full of panicked people." She shrugs. "Up to you what you want to do, but I know where we're headed."

Trish says, "To answer your other question, we were there for probably the same reason as you."

My brows lift. "You're hurt?" Neither of them looks like it on the surface.

"No, but you can't be too safe with roads blowing up and towns going into lockdown."

"Are you two from here? Do you know what happened to make the place burn down?"

"We're not from anywhere. We wander here and there, but yeah, we're familiar with this place," Trish says.

Molly adds, "I'm sure there were plenty of people with the same idea about supplies. It doesn't take a genius to put two and two together."

"It could've just been an accident..."

"Sure. So could the roads all exploding, one after the other—spontaneous combustion, right?" She gives a dark laugh. "Whatever makes you sleep at night, Ben."

We hear the sonic boom of the fighter jets before we see them. The sound is so loud while on the open pavement I fear for my eardrums. The windows on homes and buildings rattle in their frames, and even small pebbles on the ground vibrate. They're gone before I can blink.

My first thought is *about damned time*, but then it hits me—fighter jets are frickin' military. Why the hell would the military need to fly overhead? *There's a base not too far away...they could be training...but something tells me that's not what this is.*

The three of us share a knowing look as we turn onto a side street, hoping the houses that are a little deeper inside town are left more intact. *Eenie meenie miney moe... which one looks like it has the most groceries in the fridge?*

Am I really doing this again?

Looks like it.

Molly and Trish steer us toward a dark-blue two-story with a front porch. It looks so *welcoming*, like if I knocked at the door, a friendly face would smile and invite us in for a cup of coffee. *It's a house Rachel would love.*

"Are you sure?" Trish whispers.

Molly nods before twisting the door handle. It opens freely. Inside, we head straight for the kitchen, and to my delight, food fills both the fridge and pantry, and these people have good taste. I grin. "You guys were right."

"Of course we were." Molly smiles. "You didn't think we didn't know what we were talking about, did you?"

Filling my plate and pockets, I catch sight of a TV in the living room. *Worth a try...*

The screen changes from black to gray, and just when I think it's about to show nothing but static, an emergency news broadcast flashes across the screen. At the sight of it and the sound of the matching siren warning, the plate I'm holding falls.

STAY INSIDE. DO NOT LEAVE YOUR HOME. KEEP WINDOWS CLOSED. LOCK THE DOORS.

Holy shit. Lock the doors— Without meaning to, I turn toward the stairs. *There could be people here. They're hiding and we broke into their home to steal their food.* The thought freezes me.

I don't know what to do. Do I search them out? Try to talk to them, to apologize—or do I just leave?

The door wasn't locked. It was open.

I turn the TV back off. If they didn't know they had an intruder, they sure as shit do now. "I'm sorry. We didn't know," I say to the room. *I might be wrong. There might be no one here at all...*

Straining to listen, I squint my eyes and hold my breath to focus. *Was that a creak?* Just the house settling or one of the ladies in the kitchen.

"What's wrong?" Trish whispers behind me.

I jump at her sudden appearance. "God, you know how to sneak up on someone, don't you?"

"Sorry. I heard a crash."

"Did you hear the TV, too?"

She frowns and nods. "Yeah."

"What the hell, Trish? Did you guys know?" I lower my voice to barely a breath. "Are there people here?"

Her eyes flash toward the stairs and back. Something stirs behind her brown eyes—gears turning as she considers. "Maybe," she finally answers. "But if there are, we're not bothering them and they're not bothering us. We're only here for food, and we'll go."

Something about that just doesn't sit right with me. It's like she doesn't *care* if there's anyone here or not. It makes no difference. "I can't—" I start to shake my head. I don't know what I'm going to say, though. That I can't eat someone's food if they're here? Is that even true?

My pockets weigh heavy while the shattered mess on the floor stares up at me. *Don't lie, Ben. You'd eat the entire fridge if you had a chance.* But with them home? Right under their noses while I leave them with nothing?

My stomach growls.

I'm going to drive myself crazy. I pick up the mess I made and, ending our conversation, I move back to the kitchen to fix a new plate, determined to just eat and leave, like Trish said. Whether there's someone else here or not, it's none of my business. It doesn't change the fact that I need to get home, and I need food in order to survive. *Do whatever it takes. They're not bothering me, and I'm not going to bother them.* And, no matter what happens, I'm sure as hell not going upstairs.

SIXTEEN

As we're preparing to leave, noises come from a distance. My first instinct is to look back toward the staircase, but the sound comes again, and I realize it's not coming from upstairs. It's moving from outside.

I move to the front window, ducking down out of sight as I get a better view. That's when my breath catches in my throat. There are people out there. A lot of them. There are armored trucks—

The color drains from my face. There are armed men.

"You guys have to see this," I hiss.

Molly and Trish join me at the window.

The people outside are too far away to see their faces. My captors could be among them. Or these people could be totally different.

We watch as they move down the streets, the majority sticking to Main, but many splitting off down side streets, including the one we're on.

Then someone's voice booms over a megaphone. "We are here to help," he says. "Another attack is imminent.

You are all in danger." He pauses, scanning with a set of binoculars before continuing. "Come to the safe zone. You will be protected." He waits again, then, "You are not safe here. Come to the safe zone."

The man sets the megaphone down and stands waiting. After a couple of minutes, his head swivels. Behind him, a door opens, and a family shuffles out of their house. The man welcomes them with open arms, guiding them to his men, who then lead them back to Main Street.

Another few minutes pass before another door opens, and a couple comes out. Soon, others follow suit. It's more people than I imagined were here, but still not as many as I expected. People are hesitant to trust these men. Though they look like military, armed and dressed in camo, they never claimed to be so, and it's unnerving.

Who else would they be?

"Who do you think they are?" I breathe.

"Looks like military to me," Trish says, confirming my own suspicions.

"I don't know," Molly adds. "Look at the way they're moving. Something is...different."

Trish turns to her, anger flashing. "Are you so familiar with the military that you'd know how they move?"

"You know what I mean."

"Oh, I do?"

"Shh. You guys, watch," I say.

There's something about the way the people out there are looking through windows, eyes shifting from house to house, scanning the environment. The way they're spread out through the streets. *Like a pack of predators. Wolves dressed as sheep...*

They're not hurting anyone. In fact, they're doing the opposite. They're more than just guiding people to their trucks. They're offering bottled water and first aid kits and looking friendly while doing so.

The sight of so many people going to them for aid has me relieved. I banish the reservations in the back of my mind, even daring to smile. It's going to be fine. Jack was wrong. Whoever they are, they're just trying to help.

Trish and Molly seem to feel the same. The three of us move from the window when there's more movement. And this time it is from upstairs. A woman and her child stand hand in hand at the top of the staircase.

"Shit," Trish whispers.

Molly grabs hold of her hand, squeezes it, and calls up to the woman, repeating my words from earlier. "We're sorry. We didn't know anyone was home."

As they descend without a word, the woman's eyes don't leave mine. Holding her son's hand in a death grip, she moves past me to the door.

I'm stunned by the sight, by her reaction to us.

I was right!

"Wait—" I start when I finally have coherent thoughts.

The woman ignores us. She opens the front door and guides her son outside. The boy glances back through the open doorway, and I can only watch.

I should go after them—no, go with them. What am I waiting for?

"We should stop them," I say aloud, remaining frozen.

"We'll go," Molly says, pulling Trish toward the door.

"Wait, what?"

"Are you sure?" Trish asks, not hiding the hopeful gleam in her eyes. "I thought you wanted to wait?"

Molly shrugs. "We waited. Now they're right here, and there's no better time than the present."

Trish throws her arms around Molly's neck.

"Are you sure that's the best decision?" I say. "I don't think—"

What don't I think? Two seconds ago, I just told myself that everything was fine, and yet...

Smiling, Molly says, "Come with us, Ben."

"I have to get to my family. My wife probably thinks I'm dead."

"And the safe zone is probably the first place she'll look."

"Maybe. But I have to check home first."

Trish looks outside toward the woman and her son, still approaching the people—whoever they are. "We'll explain to them," she says. To Molly, she says, "Come on. If we're going, we better go."

They each nod to me and with a smile, wish me the best. I'm torn between begging them not to go and escorting them to the trucks myself. The protective side of me wants to make sure they're fine, not just because they saved my life, but because it's the right thing to do. And as much as I want to, my instincts are screaming the opposite.

Stay back. Watch and wait.

So that's what I do. Alone again, I watch Molly and Trish head down the street, attempting to catch up with the woman and her son. I hope she doesn't hold a grudge against us, and I hope what we did doesn't affect her for the rest of her life. *They'll apologize and explain. She'll understand*, I tell myself, hoping it's not a lie.

Since they're jogging, and she's not, it doesn't take long for them to catch up to her. A few words are exchanged, but it's impossible to tell if the conversation is good or bad. Trish and Molly keep going, reaching a truck, handing over their gun, and loading up even before some of the others who were waiting already.

The woman and her son are among the last people to join the group of men. Everyone is organized and filed away into trucks, the cargo doors shut and—*locked.* My eyes widen at the sight, and I'm not the only one with a knee-jerk reaction to hide.

Some of the last remaining, who haven't yet been loaded into a truck, start to distance themselves. A couple shake their heads and turn to return to their homes. One of the armed men reaches out to grab hold of a woman, and that's when all hell breaks loose.

It's too far to hear the words but not to hear the tone of the shouts. The demeanor of the armed men changes in a heartbeat. No longer friendly and welcoming, they're now demanding, pointing their assault rifles in people's faces. A shot goes off. People scream, try to run.

I watch helplessly as more shots are fired. The door is still open. If I move to close it, will they see me? *Shit, shit, shit!*

The armed group branches off again, fanning into side streets, and when I see the first door kicked in, something inside unfreezes. I can't just stand here and watch. I have to go; I have to get the hell out of this town because they're coming for me.

My heart hammers into overdrive as I look for a back

door to sneak through. In the rear of the house, there's a sliding glass door leading to the backyard. I slip through into the fenced yard, listening to the sounds of more doors caving in.

"Found one!" a man calls, followed by the sound of a child's cries.

I race to the wooden slats of the fence to see a boy being yanked by his hair down the sidewalk across the street. The child's mother races after, screaming at the top of her lungs. "No! Leave him alone!" She follows the man, beating her fists against his back, yanking at his clothes and bulletproof vest. "You bastard! Leave him!"

Her pleas freeze in her throat when he rounds on her and puts a bullet in her chest. Blood sprays from her chest and back as the bullet enters and exits her body. She drops. The boy screams incoherent cries, reaching for his mother. The man adjusts his hold in his hair and continues pulling.

I move away from the fence facing the front street, pushing farther into the back corner of the yard where a garden shed sits. Behind the shed, the fence is rotting. I stay as low as I'm able, but with my leg and other injuries, it's only a matter of time before I'm noticed.

Don't think about it. Just keep going!

Walking through the backyard gate would lead me right out onto the street into their waiting arms. So instead, I go through the fence, ripping at the rotted wood until one of the slats yanks free.

Blood rushing in my ears, sweat pouring out of me, my face twisted in agony, I try to listen to my surroundings. The screaming, shattering, and occasional gunfire are enough to mask the sound of another wooden slat coming free. A quick glance through to the neighboring yard, then I step through. My stomach gets stuck. I suck it in, squeeze—*fuck!* I wrench another board off the fence to fit the rest of the way through.

The noise of the final board coming off is like a gunshot through the air. *Or was that an actual gunshot?* The sound was so close I can't tell. I don't stop to find out.

I move to the front of this yard, which faces another side street. When I peek through the gate, I see a couple of armed men and women, but not nearly as many. There's a split second for me to choose—go through the gate or go into the house. If someone behind me heard the fence, I only have moments before they start looking through the yards.

Through the gate…or through the house? Gate or house!

I reach for the latch on the gate.

SEVENTEEN

As I pass through to the front yard, sounds come from inside the house. A door busting in. *More screaming.*

My crutch gets caught in the bushes as I start to rush across the street. *Come on, come on!* I could scream my frustration.

More men with guns are coming closer. I hold my breath, waiting for them to pass, then when they're down the street far enough, I leave the crutch and run. Luckily there's enough adrenaline pumping through me to get my ass moving despite the pain.

Street after street, I run, duck, hide, wait. I don't know how much time passes while I move through town, keeping hidden while watching them take people from their homes. They don't get everyone, but they get enough. I'm far from the trucks but close enough to hear them start up, to hear the people inside banging against the walls for their freedom, to hear the silence left behind.

Body after body line Main Street. Dead. Lined up side by side to face anyone daring to enter or exit town. When I see them there, blood flowing into the pavement like a red river, I lose control of my stomach. The vomit comes sudden and violent until there's nothing left to spit up.

The only thought running through my mind is of my family. Rachel, Ryan, Bea. *Are they okay? Are they safe?* Did these people come to my home too? Did they take my wife and kids the way they took the people here?

I have to get home to them.

Molly, Trish, the woman from the house, and her son —their faces haunt me. They walked with open arms into those trucks. And I let them. I just stood there and watched, knowing I had reservations, knowing something inside me doubted what we were seeing. I ignored my instincts and did nothing.

I leave, never once looking back. Home is only a handful of miles away. By tonight, I'll be there. I'll stay up all night walking if that's what it takes.

When I'm in the forest, I reach into my pocket for some of the painkillers. It won't be long before I crash off the adrenaline, and when that happens, I'm going to wish I was unconscious. I'm also going to wish I had another crutch or a place to lie down. I don't even want to think about the corrective surgery that looms in my future. At the rate I'm going, I may have a limp for the rest of my life.

If I ever make it out of this.

I'm going to make it home. Everything is going to be fine.

I watched the trucks head onto the highway out of town earlier, which only made me wonder about what Jack and Molly each said. *They blew up the roads.* If that's the case, where the hell are they headed?

Either way, with them on the road, I'm sticking to the forest for as long as possible. The terrain is harder to navigate, but it's worth it for the coverage. If they see me, I'll never get away again. Not with my injuries.

The day is long and agonizing. I stop for the second time for another dose of painkillers and to eat some of the snacks I managed to take from town. More than anything, I want to sit, to rest, but I don't dare because if I do, I know I won't get back up.

Something catches my attention. From the corner of my eye, a faint movement. I turn, focus, and see a barely perceptible plume of smoke between the trees. A fire. *Are you the good guys or bad?* I wonder.

The smoke is nothing like the fire from the freeway. It's so faint, it's almost invisible from where I'm standing, and it doesn't look very far away. *Almost like a campfire.*

I shiver at the memory of the last campfire—the one my captors built. Jack. Poor Jack and everything he went through. He didn't deserve the end he got. Not falling and being crushed and not being shot. "I'm sorry, Jack," I whisper. I don't think he really would've shot me, but I guess I'll never know for sure.

Is it them again? I wonder at the smoke. My captors followed me all this way. They weren't with those armed men in town as far as I could tell, but they're here now, waiting for me to approach like a dumb ass.

But what if it's not them? What if it's other people like me, who have no idea what the hell is going on? They've started a fire, and those men out there are just looking for a sign. That fire is like a beacon, shining the way, saying, "Hey, guys! We're over here!"

I have to find out one way or another.

As carefully and quietly as I'm able, I head in the direction of the smoke. When I'm close enough to hear voices, I wait to listen, and I know almost immediately these people aren't the same men who dragged me from sleep in the hunting cabin.

"How long are we going to stay here, Jace?" a woman says.

"We'll head out tomorrow. The safe zone isn't far," a man, Jace, I'm assuming, replies.

"What about East Elk? We could stop there for the night," a second woman says.

"They got hit too," Jace says. "It's not safe anywhere but the forest."

"They're right, Jace. We're starving here when there's a town not far from us," another man says.

There's a whole group of these people, and they don't know about the danger they're walking into. When I've heard enough to know they're not a threat to me, I decide I have to warn them.

I come forward, no longer bothering to be quiet, and hoping that my noise actually warns them of my presence so they're not blindsided when I step out.

One of the men calls out, "Who's there?"

"I'm Ben," I say. "I'm a friend." A moment later, I reach the group of three men, three women, and two kids that look to be young teens. They all eye me warily, two holding pistols aimed my way.

"You can't go to East Elk," I say.

One of the men raises his eyebrows, and when he speaks, I recognize his voice as the one they called Jace. "Why not?" he asks.

"I just came from there. There were people, armed to the teeth, taking people from their homes." I shake my head. "I don't think the *safe zone* is as safe as they say."

One of the women speaks up. "You don't *think*? What proof do you have?"

I frown at her tone. "They were trying to get people to come out of their homes—to take them to the safe zone. Then they *killed* them."

She purses her lips.

Another woman speaks. "They killed everyone?"

"No—"

"I think you need to get your facts straight here." Anger flares in her cheeks. "You're making these people out to be murderers when you're full of contradictions."

My jaw grinds together as I attempt to keep my anger in check. If I blow up at these people, there's no way they're going to listen. I take a deep breath before saying, "Please, lady. I'm trying to tell you—these people *are* murderers. What does it matter if they killed everyone or not? What matters is that they were ripping people from their homes, and they killed even *one*—"

"Listen," one of the men says. "Talk like this is going to scare everyone."

"Good. You should be scared."

The woman speaking earlier throws up her arms and walks away. "I can't talk to him," she says.

I turn to Jace, the one who seems like he might have somewhat more authority. "Please," I plead. "Don't let your people go into that town or to that safe zone."

He stares at me for a moment before responding. "How did you find us?"

"The smoke from your fire. You should put it out, and we should all move." I know I'm pushing my luck with these people, but better to tell them everything while they hate me already.

"This guy is joking," the woman who *couldn't talk to me* says.

"I'm not. Those men are out there, hunting people down. They'll see the smoke just like I did, and it won't take them long. Mark my words."

"What, are you a profit now? Here to give us your mighty warning?"

I hold up my hands while taking a step back. I look around at the group, noting how each of them, even the kids, looks at me with disdain. *What the hell did I say that was wrong?* "I'm sorry," I say. "I didn't mean to come at you on the wrong foot. I just—" I take another deep breath. "I overheard part of your conversation as I was passing by, and I had to warn you. I watched people get murdered—"

My throat closes on itself, unable to recount the exact memory of what happened earlier in the day. I want to say *I'm lucky to be alive,* but the words won't come. A few of the group softens when they see me choking on my own words, but others still don't want to listen.

"You have no idea how long we've been out here," one of the women says. "We're just trying to get to safety."

I nod. "I know. Me too."

"Aren't we all?" Jace says. He puts a hand on my shoulder. "Sit with us. You look like you need a rest." He nods to my bloody pant legs.

"Thank you. But I can't. I'm telling you, those people—"

"Enough!" the woman who hates me screams.

I cringe, not from the single word speared at me but from the echo her voice causes. Birds fly from the tree-tops, scattering into the sky. *Pinpointing our exact location.*

Another look to each of their faces tells me I'm doing nothing but wasting my voice and my time.

You tried. Let them talk it out.

I hope that they do.

"I'll go," I say. I turn from the group, heading back into the forest without a word of protest from any of them.

EIGHTEEN

Such a waste of time. I can't help but be angry with myself for getting distracted trying to be some kind of hero. What made me think anyone would listen? Of course they're not going to take the word of some random injured stranger walking out of the forest. They probably think I'm either crazy or one of the baddies.

Frustrated more with myself for wasting time trying than with them for not listening, I head back the way I came, so I can continue in the same direction the road takes. Voices erupt behind me as I step away from the group. They argue among themselves, actually taking what I said into consideration.

It surprises me, but I'm glad I got through to at least a few of them. The idea of them being victims to those people sends chills down my spine.

That's exactly why I tried to convince them.

My temper begins to ease when I hear someone call

I spin back around to see Jace jogging to catch up with me.

"Don't go yet," he says. "I'm sorry we were so rude."

"No. It doesn't matter. I'm just trying to keep anyone else from getting killed."

"It's just—we're all tired and scared, and seeing you" —he motions toward my injuries—"it really freaked some of us out."

My eyebrows dip down. "I'm trying to warn you guys so this doesn't happen to any of you."

"We know." He sighs. "Please, will you come back? A few of us have some questions."

I hesitate. *What other questions could there possibly be? Either they're going to put out the fire and move or they're not...*

Reluctantly I take a step toward him. "I'll answer what I can, but I'm serious when I say time is an issue here."

Jace nods. "Understood."

When we return to the others, I notice the fire put out, and it brings a wave of relief. These people may have acted like they didn't want to hear a word I was saying, but in less than five minutes, they actually did take my warning to heart. *Maybe it wasn't such a waste of time after all.*

Jace looks around the group before addressing them. "He took a chance warning us. He didn't have to do that." He turns back to me. "Thanks, man." He holds out his hand to shake. "I'm Jace."

"Ben," I say, shaking his hand. "I see you put the fire out. That's good. What questions did you all have? We should get going right away."

The woman whose last nerve I scratched earlier steps

forward. "Ben, I'm Heidi. I want to know, if these people are so dangerous, how did you make it out alive? Are you really here to warn us, or are you here for something else?"

I look to Jace, who gives me a nod with a faint smile, then back to Heidi. Her open, unblinking stare is unnerving and irritating. How can she look at the condition I'm in and actually ask me these questions with a serious face?

"I hid, and I ran," I say simply. "And I'm not going to stand around trying to convince you I'm trustworthy. We've wasted enough time."

"So you expect us to just take your word at face value?"

"Yes," I ground out. "Look at me, lady. I'm damn near *broken*. I made the effort to be a good person, I came back when I can hardly walk as it is, and now I'm standing here arguing with you when I should be getting far the hell away from here before those assholes show up." I take a step away from the group. "I need to get to my family. I don't have time for this."

"We all want our families," Jace says.

"We just want to make sure we're doing the right thing," someone else says.

The sound of nearby engines makes me freeze. For a split second, I think my mind might be playing tricks on me. *Those aren't engines. They're something else. I'm hearing things, imagining those people coming to find us because I'm so goddamned scared.* But it's them alright. They're getting closer by the second.

"We have to run," I breathe, barely able to form the words.

Shock and alarm register on most of the other's faces, but there are still some who don't fully understand what's about to happen. *There's no more time to explain to them.*

"I thought you said they took off down the road toward the safe zone?" Heidi says, arching her eyebrows at me.

"They did. I don't know—"

"Again with the not knowing!" she cries, looking around the group. "Look, this could be someone else. We have no way of knowing whoever it is means us any harm. Maybe it's *real* help."

"Are you really going to stick around and find out?" I demand.

"He's right," one of the other women says. She stands close to the kids, pulling them close to her chest. "We need to get out of here while we can."

"And go where?" someone else says.

"Anywhere! We can take cover in the trees." I'm the first to move, but no one follows. Hurried whispers come from the group again. I keep going as fast as I'm physically able.

I ignore my body's cries of agony, begging me to slow down and rest. If I hadn't been in East Elk, I'd probably be like them, probably doubt the danger. Hell, I *did* doubt it when Jack tried to tell me. But then I was there. I saw what they did, and nothing anyone says is going to change that. I know what these people are capable of.

Minutes later, the engines turn off.

I push myself harder, silently hoping I blend in with my surroundings. I'm too far to see the group now, but I can hear the deep baritone of men's voices having a discussion. *Keep going! Not far enough!*

A few moments later, a woman shouts. *Was that Heidi?* I cringe, expecting gunshots or more yelling, but none come.

My surprise makes me slow and look back. Doubt begins to worm its way in like a slippery eel. *Was I wrong?*

There's another scream. More yelling. Then the guns.

Something in my leg cracks when I run, almost bringing me to my knees. I look down at myself, seeing the trail of blood I've been leaving behind. *Well, isn't that perfect?* Gritting my teeth to keep from passing out, I tie off my bleeding leg again, pop a couple more painkillers, and move.

Sweat drips down into my eyes, salt stinging my vision. My arms move between clearing my sight and clearing the low branches from smacking me in the face as I move. My eyes dart everywhere—down to keep from falling, back to see if I've been seen, and all around as my desperation intensifies.

I'm never going to outrun them. Not in a million years. Not in my condition, and not even if I didn't have a scratch on me.

The best chance I have is to find a good hiding spot and pray they don't have dogs that will sniff me out.

More gunshots. More screaming. Closer, now. Someone running.

Shit!

They're coming toward me—probably will run right into me the way my slow ass is moving.

Not enough pep in the step this time...

I change course, turning left and right, weaving a different path than I was taking. That's when I spot my salvation.

A massive tree stares at me, with a cavity at least four

feet tall. There's no time to think about it. It's either this or keep running, and I choose this.

I duck down and push my body into the opening. When my stomach catches against the bark, I suck in and force myself in farther. I brush against spider webs, grimacing as they touch my face and skin. *A spider wouldn't crawl into an open wound, would it?*

I banish the thought. *Thinking like that is not helpful right now!*

There's not much other foliage to block the opening, but luckily, I'm able to tuck myself in against the inside of the trunk. There's enough room to hide myself without a passerby noticing me. They'd have to stick their head inside the opening to see me.

A walkie-talkie buzzes nearby. "Anything yet?" a voice says.

I almost jump out of my skin at the proximity. He's so close I can hear him draw in a breath before responding.

"He's close."

Shit.

What was I thinking? That they wouldn't investigate a tree hollow this big? They'd just waltz right on by, like, *oh no there wouldn't be any idiots hiding in there!*

My heart thrums, blood pulsing down to my finger-tips, ears ringing, my whole body feels like it's on fire. Pins and needles are bursting out of my pores, and I feel like I could easily piss myself if I'm not careful.

What have I got myself into?

Two seconds later, footsteps are right outside the tree opening.

This is it—

A man leans down inside. He scans the darkness

then, eyes finally landing on me, he grins. "Well, well, what have we here?"

A gunshot rings out.

I close my eyes.

I wait, expecting more pain to hit me any second—there's a thud. My eyes fly open to see the man dropped, his eyes bulging, and blood flowing freely from a gunshot wound. Someone is dragging him backward.

"You okay in there?" a voice calls.

"H-Heidi?"

"I'm not sure who that is, but it's not me."

I wait while whoever it is clears the man from the entrance. When the opening is clear, I make my way back out of the tree, trying not to cry out every time my full weight rests on my injuries. A hand reaches to help me, and I take it gratefully, so focused on the pain in my body, I don't care who it is.

When I finally have hold of myself, I look to see a short blonde woman carrying a rifle.

"I'm Tammy," she says. "We better get the hell out of here."

NINETEEN

I follow Tammy's lead without question, only knowing that she just saved my life and that she's helping me stand. At this point, without her help, I'd fall on my ass again, and thankfully she doesn't seem to mind supporting me. It feels weird being almost twice her size in both height and weight, but she's much stronger than she looks.

"Were those your people?" she asks at one point.

"No. I was trying to warn them."

"You stayed too long."

"You think?"

She gives me a look at my sarcasm.

"I'm sorry," I say.

Tammy is silent for a moment before saying, "I take it they didn't listen."

"Basically."

She nods. "They're counting on that. On people not wanting to believe they're actually doing what they're doing."

"And what exactly are they doing?" I ask.

"You mean you don't know?" she says, eyebrows raised.

"I think I do, but all I really know is what I saw—they're out there killing people."

"They kill the ones who don't go with them," she says.

"You mean some of those people back there could still be alive?"

Tammy nods. "If they went willingly, then yes, most likely."

"Where are they taking them? The safe zone?"

"Yeah. And the people going there on their own are walking into a trap."

"I don't understand who the hell these people are. Why would they want to trap a bunch of people like that? For what purpose?"

"Have you noticed there's no emergency response? No police, EMT, military, nothing."

"That's exactly what I've noticed, yes! Except, there were fighter jets that flew overhead. Did you hear them in East Elk?"

"Those were mostly for show, and yes, they're probably doing a lot of things in the background, but there's a bigger picture here. It's because we're in a hostage situation. And, in a hostage situation, there's a certain amount of time to negotiate before they all get their heads blown off.

"Whoever these people are, they know what they're doing. They're using all the people they can as leverage to get whatever they want while they have the upper hand. But they also know time is running out and the more people that need to be rescued, the more likely they are to get what they want."

We stop next to a large boulder, where Tammy helps me lean against it as we both catch our breath. Everything she's saying makes sense—sort of. But how the hell does she know it all? How would she know what they're up to when no one else seems to?

"I have a truck hidden not far away," she says.

I look up at that, startled. "You what?"

She sighs. "I saw you in East Elk. I saw what happened to those people and I followed you. Then I saw you talking to the group. I wasn't trying to spy, but I thought if I popped out after the way you did, those people really would've had a fit."

"You acted like you didn't know what I said to them."

Tammy shrugs. "Just making conversation. Come on, we need to move." She ducks under my armpit, wrapping her arm around my waist before I can protest.

As we continue, I ask, "So what now? What do we do?"

"I don't know about you, but the first thing I want is to get far the hell away."

"I-I can't do that."

She seems startled by my words, so I add, "I was on the freeway when there was an explosion. I've been trying to get home for days—my family probably thinks I'm dead. I need to get home to make sure they're safe."

Tammy purses her lips. "Where do you live? The roads are hell, as I'm sure you know."

"Welldeer. It's only a few miles west of East Elk. I have to get to my family, Tammy, roads or no roads."

She thinks for a second before nodding. "Okay. I can drop you off but then I'm out of there. I have nothing and no one holding me back, and I'm not playing the damsel in distress game. You get me?"

"I get you. And I don't blame you for one second. I owe you my life already."

A blush creeps up Tammy's cheeks and neck, but she doesn't say anything else. I don't know what luck I had to put me in her path, but I'm sure as hell thankful. For the first time in days, I'm going to be in a vehicle again, not forced to walk or push my injured body to the breaking point. I'll see my family in a matter of minutes.

Just like she said, Tammy's truck isn't far away. She has a camo tarp, along with a bunch of leaves and twigs thrown over the top, making it blend into the forest so well, I almost don't see it at all. Tammy rips off the tarp to reveal an older two-door gray Dakota with peeling paint.

"Are they going to hear us start it up?" I ask.

"She's pretty quiet, but maybe. Come on." She opens the passenger door and helps me inside before rushing around to her own side. Moments later, the truck is purring like a kitten, and we're off.

T ammy drives slowly, weaving in and out of trees, seeming to know exactly where she's going. As she navigates, my eyes keep darting to the side mirror and window to watch for anyone following. We're being quiet, but are we quiet enough to go unnoticed?

Something tells me no. Those people are looking for

us, listening. They won't miss a truck driving through the forest. It's just a matter of time before—

"Shit! Tammy, we've got a problem!" I cry, watching in horror as a white truck pulls behind us.

"I see it," Tammy says before flooring the gas pedal.

The engine roars, and we surge forward. I yell incoherent profanity as she dodges tree after tree. When we get to a straight stretch, Tammy holds one hand on the steering wheel and reaches behind my seat with the other.

"Take this," she says, handing me her rifle.

"Gladly," I say with false confidence. I'd love to shoot these assholes, but I also don't know what I'm doing, and I'll probably wind up shooting our own tailgate.

Rolling down the window, I try to twist in my seat to get good aim, but any way I position myself is painful. The rifle is too big, the cab too small, and with all the jostling, I'll never get a good aim.

"What are you waiting for?" Tammy cries. "Shoot them!"

My hold on the gun tightens. She's right. *Suck it up, Ben.*

Fighting past the pain and discomfort, I lean out the window with the rifle.

The truck immediately veers right, anticipating a shot. I squeeze the trigger, bracing against the sound and the recoil. A bullet pings off something—what, I have no idea. I keep squeezing the trigger, one pop after another.

The truck continues dodging, and it doesn't take long for one of the passengers to return fire.

"They're probably a better shot than I am, Tammy," I warn.

"Keep trying!" she says, and the look she gives me, full of fear of helplessness, makes me determined to blow the tire out from under those fuckers. This woman saved my life, and I'm sitting here complaining about how uncomfortable I am and about how bad a shot.

Taking a deep breath to steady myself, I lean back out the window and shoot again. Aim, brace, squeeze, repeat. I go through almost an entire magazine, but it doesn't matter, because when I see that puff of air from the front tire, I know I hit my mark.

They keep rolling until the rubber falls from the rim, and the truck slows to a crawl. I laugh, watching the driver yelling at the passenger, throwing his hands in the air, looking like he could throttle the man. Tammy whoops and cheers at our success. She's focused on getting us back out of the forest, onto the road. She doesn't see what I see.

We're almost too far away from the truck to see inside, but not quite. Still laughing at the driver's anger, I haven't turned back around in my seat yet. That's when he takes out a pistol and shoots the passenger.

The laughter dies in my throat. That man just died because he wasn't able to stop us.

TWENTY

"**D**ammit, this is worse than when Rainier erupted," Tammy says, navigating the truck along the burned and broken highway. We go for a few miles unhindered until hitting a stretch of half-melted pavement riddled with potholes and broken-down cars. She turns to me. "We might have to get out and walk."

"Whatever we need to do," I say, dreading the thought of walking again. I roll my ankle, testing the muscles in the leg that's the worst off. That small motion alone is agony, not just to my leg but to the rest of my broken body.

"One good thing," Tammy says. "Is if we can't get through this, I'm sure they can't either. I bet your family is safe and sound." She gives me a reassuring smile before tapping our bumper against another car.

"Shit." she shifts into reverse. When we've cleared the blockage, she shifts back into drive to go around, but there's more debris blocking the way. We back up and try again, and again until Tammy finally slams her hands on the sides of the steering wheel, eyes blazing.

"It's okay. We're close anyway," I say. And it's true. I can see the turnoff for the main road from here. It's probably only three or four football fields away.

"Come on, let's go before it gets dark."

We shuffle out of the truck. Tammy looks almost comical, wedged between me on one side and the rifle almost as big as she is on the other. She frowns over at me as I limp my way along and it's clear we're not going to be able to keep this up for very long. Running for our lives in the forest is one thing, but this is another.

I don't know why she doesn't complain or leave me to fend for myself. She'd have every right to worry about her own survival before mine, and not only that, but to not put herself through the torment of lugging me around. The amount of strength this woman possesses is staggering.

"I'm going to look for something for you to lean on," she says, finally needing a break. She lets go of me to search through some of the burned-up cars.

I wait for her, doubting she'll be able to find anything useful that's not scorched. "See if you can find a phone while you're looking," I call, suspecting she won't find one of those either.

Minutes pass as I watch her continue down the broken road. *How long is she going to do this?* I wonder. Then, before much longer, she heads back to me, a triumphant smile on her face—a *shovel* in her hand.

"You're joking," I say when she holds it over her head like some kind of trophy.

"Nope. Look at it—it's perfect! And not burned because it's *steel*."

"It's a...shovel."

"*Garden spade*," she insists. "Look at the narrow blade. It's perfect."

"Okay... I don't know how you know about tools, but the point I'm trying to make is *look* at it, Tammy. It might not be burned, but the damn thing needed to be replaced a hundred years ago. I'm going to need to put *significant* weight on it." I lift my eyebrows, hoping she catches my meaning without me having to spell out the words. I'm heavy, and this thing would be fine if I wasn't so completely broken and if it didn't look like it came from World War II.

Tammy purses her lips. "I know what you're thinking," she says. "I think it's stronger than it looks, Ben." She slaps the blade against the pavement, testing its strength.

To my surprise, the thing holds up well to her hammering it repeatedly against the asphalt. Good enough for me anyway. I hold out my hand for it, and as much as I don't like the thing, I'm glad to have it.

A couple of hours later, we're turning off the main road onto my cul-de-sac. My pulse races as we walk through the small town of Welldeer, much smaller than East Elk. It's normal for things to be dead most days. Not very many cars on the road or traffic going through town. There aren't any big-name stores, only small businesses trying to carve their way in the world.

There's something about this kind of dead that's a little *too* dead though. Tammy and I remain silent as we approach my front door. Dread worms its way into my heart with every step.

"Rach?" I call just outside the front door. I turn the door handle—locked. I reach in my pockets for the keys — "Shit! I left them in the truck." My face flames. *How could I have forgotten the damned house keys?*

"Is there a back door?" Tammy asks.

"Yeah, but chances are, that one's locked too."

"I'll check it out." She takes off around the back, leaving me to pound on the front door like an angry ex.

"Rach! It's me! I'm home!" I try again. No creaking floorboards, no shadow passing in front of the window, no voices calling back to me—no answer.

My throat closes in on itself, robbing me of air. I double over, the spade falling to my feet as I hyperventilate. *This isn't happening. They're here. They're safe.*

The dead bolt unlocks.

I stand, but before I can reach for my wife, all hope is extinguished. Tammy stands inside my doorway with a sheepish smile. "Sorry," she says, standing back. "Had to let myself in."

Moving past her to the stairs, I call for my wife and kids again, pushing past the pain to climb the steps. "I'm alive, you guys. It's okay! Say something, anything!"

I search the entire top floor before moving back downstairs and then the garage. The whole time I'm trying to hold myself together, trying to keep from having another panic attack. Only when I've searched every inch do I finally accept what's staring me in the face.

"They're gone."

"Do you have a house phone? Maybe—"

"No."

"We could try one of the neighbors?"

I brighten slightly at that. "It's worth a shot."

Tammy follows me as I knock on door after door around the cul-de-sac. Only one answers, looking at me as if I've lost my mind. My family isn't here.

"Why haven't you gone to the safe zone yet?" my neighbor asks. "That's where almost everyone else is."

"Listen to me, Shelly. You can't go there. It's not safe!" I cry, startling her. She takes a step back inside, almost closing the door on my face.

"I'm sorry," I say, rushing to add. "I saw those people and what they're doing. Please, you have to believe me. It's not as safe as they'd have you believe."

She glares at me. "You do you, and I'll do me," she says, then she closes the door the rest of the way.

I turn to Tammy, defeated. "We have to find them, Tam. I-I need your help."

Tammy nods. "We're going to find them." She wraps an arm around one of mine, leading me back home. "Come on, we better get inside."

TWENTY-ONE

The long night gives me an opportunity to get cleaned up and re-dress my bandages. After raiding the medicine cabinet, I also find a few outdated pill bottles that are much stronger than the painkillers I've been taking. In the hall closet rests my son's old set of crutches from when he broke his leg in soccer. I gladly trade my garden spade in for the upgrade. I'm as fixed up as I'm going to get—everything I need in hand, except my family.

Tammy is resting on the couch when I come downstairs. "You think they're taking care of people?" I ask. "I mean, I know they're hostages, but—you wouldn't kill hostages, right? Not once they're there?" I banish the image of all those innocent people murdered.

"I'm sure they want to keep as many alive and healthy as they can. If they start killing everyone off, they're going to lose all negotiating power."

I clear my throat as I gather my thoughts. I've never felt so helpless in my life, unable to take care of my family, and they probably really think I'm dead at this point. I turn from Tammy, so she doesn't see me squeeze my eyes shut, blocking out the thought of my children held as hostages. Ryan, my big strong teen, and my little Bea, barely starting school this year.

"Hey—" Tammy clears her throat. "You okay, Ben?"

"How are we going to do this? Are you—" I wave my hands around, gesticulating toward the door. "No one else was with you in East Elk?"

"No. Just me." She frowns. "It might just be two of us, but we'll be less noticeable. We can hide and watch for an opening."

I run my hands through my hair, willing my frayed nerves to give it a rest so I can think. Tammy's right, again, of course. I can't focus. I can't plan anything like this. These are the lives of my wife and children, not to mention countless others that are bound to be there—

"What if they're not there?" I ask.

"Where else would they be? Do they have somewhere to go?"

"No...but what if—what if Rach took the kids out looking for me? What if—"

Tammy watches me as I trail off.

"What if they're already dead because Rachel wouldn't go willingly?"

"Hey, you can't think like that, Ben."

"I know. God, I know, okay? It's just—" I hobble away on my crutch, leaving the thought left unfinished. Her positivity is killing me, when all I want to do is scream from the rooftops. Tammy is right about one thing though—we can be much less noticeable with just the two of us.

And these lovely crutches? I look down at myself,

cleaned up but still broken. I don't know how I'm moving at all. Adrenaline, I suppose, but what happens when it finally wears off? Shouldn't I have depleted my internal supply by now? What happens when I finally crash and can't get back up, and my family is right there within reach, but there's nothing I can do to help them?

I need to rest. I need a full night's sleep. I need— How in the hell am I going to sleep knowing they're gone? Can my kids sleep wherever they're at? On the ground, in the cold? Did they separate them? Take them from Rachel?

My fist slams into the wall.

Tammy jumps in surprise but doesn't speak.

"I'm sorry. I'm just—so lost," I choke.

"We need to sleep," she says as if she's read my mind. "Don't tell me you can't because when I look at you, I see a fucking zombie, Ben. In the morning, we'll go. We're going to find the safe zone and figure this thing out."

I give a slow nod. "Okay. I'll be—" I start to say upstairs but realize it might be a better idea to take it easy on my injuries as much as possible. "Why don't you take one of the kid's rooms upstairs, and I'll take the guest bedroom down here."

"Yell if you need me," Tammy says.

I could almost laugh at the irony of her—a virtual stranger helping me in my own home.

I pass out the second my head hits the pillow, and I sleep like the dead. At one point during the night, I'm not sure if I'm dreaming or not when there's pounding at the door. As hard as I try to pull myself out of sleep, I can't. That is—until Tammy shakes my shoulder and yells my name in my ear.

I sit up bolt right. "What's wrong?" I ask, vision blurry.

"There's someone pounding on the door." She holds up her rifle, moving to the window to peek through the blinds.

"Who is it?"

"Can't tell. Looks like—some guy."

"Just one? Is he armed?"

"Just one, and I'm not sure."

I shift, easing my legs out of bed as gently as I can before standing. My entire body is stiff and sore. More than sore. "Let me borrow that gun."

Tammy hands it over without hesitation and I move to the front door. One more shake of my head to clear the sleep, then I open it.

"Jesus, Ben, took you long enough!" Keith, one of my neighbors, cries. "Shelly said you came by looking for Rachel and the kids."

"What the hell, Keith? It's the middle of the damned night."

"I know. Can I come in? I'll explain."

I step back so Keith can enter, then I lock the door and hand Tammy back her rifle. A quick introduction later, we're sitting in the living room, listening to the story about the argument Keith and his wife had after we left earlier.

"She wants to go, but I know better, and after you stopped by—I was taking a shit, by the way. She didn't even want to tell me it was you or what you wanted. Can you believe that?" He scowls his disgust with his wife. "Anyway," he continues. "When I finally got it out of her, I knew there was no way in hell we were going there. I don't care what they're handing out to people or how safe it's supposed to be. No fucking way." Keith shakes his head for emphasis, crossing his arms over his chest.

"Alright, so why are you here?" I say.

He gives me a knowing look. "Well, I came to tell you I'm sorry I missed you, and I feel for you, your family missing and all. But mostly, I came to tell you I know where this place is, and I can help get you there so you can save them."

Leave it to Keith to yammer on for twenty minutes about something that doesn't matter when he's got the most important information just sitting in the back of his mind, waiting to be dug out. "You're a lifesaver, Keith. I mean it."

Keith flushes. "Sure, I mean, it's the least I can do, being a good neighbor and all."

"Are you willing to stay with us? To help?" Tammy asks.

He stammers for a second, embarrassed to be put on the spot.

"You don't have to do that," I cut in. "You're doing enough just getting us there." I give Tammy a look, trying to convey back off a little, but she ignores me.

"We can use all the help we can get, Keith," she says,

placing a hand over his. "Ben is lost without his wife and kids. How old is his little girl?"

Keith pinches his lips closed. He nods. "You're right. I'll stay, and by god, I'll do what needs to be done. I have a handgun in the safe upstairs. I'll go get it."

"Hang on a minute, Keith. I can't ask you to risk your life like this."

"Nonsense. Call it being a Good Samaritan."

"How about a phone? Is your or Shelly's phones working? We can call someone for help—"

"All the phones are down, Ben. The FBI is the only one who can do anything now. Well, besides us, of course." He nods to Tammy and me. "I'll be back in ten minutes, then we need to come up with a plan."

TWENTY-TWO

Tammy and I pile into Keith's electric car with our two guns, food, and first aid. It's not much, but it's everything we could carry from the house and medicine cabinets. I just hope it's enough to last us until some real help shows up. The aim is that I'll have a few extra changes of bandages, and we'll all have enough food not to starve.

"So, where's this place at?" Tammy asks. She's in the front with Keith, holding her rifle like it's a lifeline.

"We have to go the long way through town to get around the wreckage, but it's basically in the forest."

"And we're supposed to get there in *this*?"

"You mean Ninety-Fifth isn't blocked?" I say at the same time, feeling like a fool for not asking Tammy to try that way when we first got to town. I was so worried about getting home I didn't even think about the long way around. We could still have her truck...

Keith ignores her comment to answer me. "When they blew up the roads, they forgot about the path less traveled." He grins and laughs. "I suppose there are enough potholes, they didn't think anyone could drive on it anyway."

"Uh, you might be wrong about that," Tammy says, staring at the passenger-side mirror.

Keith's face falls as we all look back to see the white truck on our tail. The same white truck that I blew the tire out of. Looks like they didn't have a problem getting it replaced.

"You have to go, Keith. Drive!" I yell.

The driver of the truck has the gas floored, gaining on us too fast. He's either going to ram us or try driving us off the road.

Keith punches it, maneuvering around the potholes as best he can, avoiding bottoming out or blowing out our own tires. Shots ring out behind us, a ping against the paint, and then another.

"They're shooting my car!" Keith cries.

"That's not all they'll shoot," Tammy says. "Can't this thing go any faster?"

Somehow, Keith finally gets the message loud and clear and sucks more power from the accelerator. We lurch forward again, this time dipping and bouncing as Keith slams into a hole in the road. Warnings start going off left and right.

Forward collision warning. Take immediate corrective action.

Emergency brakes activate as alarms chime and warnings flash across the dash, letting us know we're all fucked.

"Goddammit!" Keith yells, swerving again as the truck taps our rear bumper. He punches the touchscreen while slapping the shifter and punching the gas again, frantic to get us the hell going again. "Come on, you piece of shit! I said disengage!" he pleads with the thing to listen as we're almost at a dead stop.

The truck comes around the shoulder, spitting gravel and chipping Keith's windshield. "They're trying to block us," Tammy cries, lifting the rifle and taking aim out the window.

Another bullet hits us—still from behind. I peek through the back window to see a second truck about to tap us again.

Obstacle aware flashes across the dash.

"No shit, there's an obstacle!" Keith yells.

We jerk forward as we're hit, and more warnings go off. I'm grimacing, hanging on to the seat, while Tammy rolls down the window to take her first shot. One more tap on the touchscreen and Keith growls as we finally have power again. He jerks the wheel around the first truck, leading us clear off the pavement and into the forest.

"How are we going to lose them, Keith?" I ask while Tammy leans farther out to shoot behind us.

She barks a laugh. "Looks like they're going to need another new tire!"

I try not to let it hurt my pride that she was able to shoot it a hell of a lot faster than I was. "I don't think they're going to back off as easy this time," I say, watching through the back window as the second truck passes the first, plowing off the pavement and following our path into the trees.

"Just keep shooting!" Keith yells. He reaches for his handgun and practically throws it at me.

"You really want me to waste the bullets?"

"It's either that or they kill us!"

Tammy pops off another few rounds, missing as both our car and the truck continue to swerve around each other and the trees. Gripping the pistol in two sweaty palms, I lean into the window opposite her side and wait for an opportunity.

Two passengers lean on each side of the truck, returning fire. When one runs out of ammo, I take my chance when he ducks inside to reload. The trigger squeezes beneath my finger, the bullet going wide. Of course. "I can't aim for shit with this thing," I complain mostly to myself. I'm not big on guns, and the change in control and aim from Tammy's rifle to Keith's pistol is an adjustment.

"You better figure something out! We're running out of forest here!" Keith yells.

Tammy shoots a couple more rounds, and I watch as the windshield cracks on the truck. The driver swerves, momentarily losing control, before she takes another shot and the tire blows.

Tammy screams her triumph. "Yes! Another one bites the dust!"

The truck soon comes to a dead stop, finally allowing the distance between us to grow. I breathe, my heart racing, adrenaline coursing through every fiber of my being. *Jesus, that was close.*

I wipe my palms on my pants, leaning toward the gap in the window to gulp in cool, fresh air. My stomach is in knots, and I can tell from the look on Keith's face in the rearview mirror he had it just as bad, if not worse. The sight of Tammy still whooping like it's time to party brings a faint smile to his lips.

Keith's eyes flick behind us again. His mouth falls open as something small flies past us. I can't tell what it is, only recognize it's not a bullet—and when it hits the ground, it explodes.

There's no time to speak before the flames lick us. The blast brings us to a dead stop, flipping us like a toy, and bringing us down in a heap. Airbags go off in an instant, punching Keith and Tammy into silence.

The crunch of metal and paint, and bone, is sickening. All I can do is hang on for dear life, watching the tilt of their heads, the sway of their hair, pens falling out of Keith's cup holder, along with loose change and gum wrappers, all hitting the windshield as we roll once, twice, then finally come to a stop.

TWENTY-THREE

My head spinning and ears ringing, I crawl away from the wreck on hands and knees. Tammy is screaming in pain, holding her bruised face, tears of pain and anger flooding her eyes. Her jaw is swollen and looks like it might be broken. Keith has two black eyes but is otherwise silent.

"We need to go," he says.

I stand and collect myself while Tammy's cries die down. It takes seconds for us to clear our thoughts enough to realize—the people who chased us are here, watching us with amused smirks on their faces.

"We should shoot you where you stand for the fucking trouble you caused," one says.

Panic rises in me again. *Rachel and the kids.* An image of my kids' faces flashes before me, Ryan learning how to take care of his car, not knowing how to do an oil change. Bea, a grown woman with her big brother walking her down the aisle because her dad's not there—

"You hear what I said?" the man barks.

Keith and Tammy have their hands raised, guns dropped

to their feet. I follow suit, raising both hands in surrender. Keith's eyes are wide, petrified masses. He's shaking like a leaf, waiting for judgment because he was the driver. But do they know that? And does it really matter? Tammy and I were the ones shooting...but Tammy doesn't seem frightened at all. In fact, she seems almost comfortable.

"If you shoot us, you'll be out three perfectly good hostages," she says.

The man flashes one of his partners an amused look. "Is that so?" he asks, circling us. "So, does that mean you're going to cooperate and be a good little girl?"

Tammy's eyes flash.

"Come on, Trev, wrap it up," one of the others calls.

A group is next to the truck, repairing the front wheel. They eye us with contempt as Trev decides what to do with us.

"You're lucky I'm in a good mood," he finally says. "Let's go, folks." He raises a hand in the air, making a circular gesture. A few others step forward to pull the three of us up.

Keith looks like he wants to either fall down and cry or go out fighting. His chin wobbles as someone grabs his shirt, shoving him forward. I try to ease myself closer so I can reassure him, but the second I try, I'm shoved to the ground and kicked in my back and stomach.

"Are you trying something stupid, asshole?" a man yells.

Someone backhands Tammy as she cries out in protest.

The kicking stops. I bite back a groan as I'm pulled to my feet.

"You going to behave?" the man asks, inches from my face.

I nod.

"Good. Next time, you're done."

I try to meet Keith's or Tammy's eyes, but we're in a single file line now, and no one's looking back.

W e're inside the safe zone in less than fifteen minutes. *At least we don't have to worry about sneaking in anymore.* I wonder how many others in here were like the three of us, just trying to get by or find family when they were abducted. I also wonder how many were shot because they fought back. And maybe more pressing—why we were spared.

Molly and Trish might be here...

There are too many questions, too many ideas swirling in my mind, when there's only one that matters above all others. Is my family okay? Are they here too?

If I didn't know we were all hostages, I'd think this place was what they say it is. On the surface, no one looks abused or mistreated. Large camouflage tarps are strung between the trees, covering row after row of sleeping bags.

If it wasn't for the barbed wire and armed guards, I might've even had second guesses about what this place really is. Maybe Tammy had it all wrong...but seeing with my own eyes that we're not free to leave, cements in everything she said. We're hostages, alright. Who's going to help us now?

"You okay, Ben?" Keith asks the moment our personal guard leaves.

"Yeah. You?" I rasp.

He huffs. "God, I thought Shelly was going to kill me because of the car, but looks like someone else is going to beat her to it."

I grip his arm. "Don't say that. If they were going to kill us, they would've done it already."

"And what's going to happen when the FBI doesn't give them what they want? When they learn the hard way that it's not so easy to fuck with the government, and they decide to send a message by killing off a few innocents?"

"They already did that, Keith. They killed tons of innocents getting people here in the first place."

He frowns and nods. "Why didn't they kill us, Ben?"

I don't know. "Maybe they've killed too many already, and they know it."

Tammy joins us. "Sleeping bags are first come, first serve. They don't have an assignment system in place, and I asked about food, but they only laughed in my face."

"Did you think they were going to pamper us?" Keith says.

"No." Tammy frowns. "But I thought they'd keep us alive." Color floods her face when she realizes how that sounds. "I mean—I just thought—"

"I thought they'd have food too," I say, thinking of the supplies in the car that we were forced to leave behind. "I wonder how long these people have gone without."

The three of us move to the edge of the area, closest to

one of the perimeter walls, where an armed guard watches us. We keep going until we're out of hearing distance, but there's another guard waiting.

"We're not going to get out of their sight," I say under my breath.

"We need to be careful. They might separate us," Keith says.

Tammy barks, "What do they think we're going to do? Start a revolt?"

"Keep it down, would you?" I say, looking around. She's not even trying to be quiet.

"Are we really not even allowed to talk to each other?" She arches an eyebrow at me.

Scowling, the guard takes a step toward us. "Is there a problem over here?"

"Not at all. We're just discussing how great it feels to be kept against our will," Tammy says.

Keith looks like a deer caught in headlights when the guard raises his gun toward us, but Tammy is still smiling. I nudge her, hissing, "What the hell are you doing?" She knows just as well as I do that these people don't like sass. They could shoot her for just looking at them the wrong way, let alone causing a scene.

"Come on, Ben," she says. "It's not like they don't know we don't want to be stuck with a bunch of shit-bag murderers." She turns away from me to call toward the people in the sleeping bag area. "What do you guys say? You like being kidnapped and held at gunpoint, against your will?"

"You better shut the hell up before I make you," the guard snarls, taking another step toward Tammy.

"She's just scared," I say, trying to cover for her. I

plead with my eyes, begging her to stop whatever game she's at.

She winks at me and starts to walk away into the center of the area.

Keith and I share a confused look before following.

"Ben? Is that you?" a voice calls.

I look around with narrowed eyes, sure my ears are deceiving me. The voice comes again, louder, and that's when I see my wife gripping my kids to her chest. They're here, and they're alive.

TWENTY-FOUR

They run to me, tears streaming down all their faces, and mine too. I pull my kids close, holding them tight against my chest. "I missed you so much," I say.

Rachel clings to me too, crying, "I knew you weren't gone. I knew it."

"What happened, Rach? How'd you guys wind up in here?"

"I could ask you the same thing," she says. She looks past me to see Keith standing a few feet away. "Keith's here with you?"

"Hi, Rachel," Keith says. "We...came to rescue you." He brushes a hand through his hair, giving her an embarrassed smile.

The sound of Rachel's laugh is like music to my ears. "You guys are doing a great job, by the way," she says before kissing me.

"I hate to break up the reunion, but did you see what happened back there?" Tammy says.

"You almost got yourself killed," Keith answers. "And

probably us, right along with you. We're supposed to be getting us and as many people we can out of this situation, not making it worse."

"And how the hell do we do that, Keith? We have to test the boundaries, see what it takes to get them to react, and what they're willing to put up with."

"Well, as you can see, they're not willing to put up with much."

"I disagree. That guard may have been annoyed, but that was nothing compared to what he could've done. And—look how easy it was to draw him into us. He left his post with only a single outburst." Tammy glares at Keith, whispering, "Imagine what we could do. These people are all bark, acting big and bad with their guns, but are they really that organized?"

"Then why hasn't help come yet?"

"Because help sees those guns and has to weigh the risk of losing innocent lives. They can't trust anything other than what they see."

"She's right about the guards," a voice says, joining us.

My eyes widen when I see Jace, bruised, with a broken nose. "Ben, I was an idiot not to listen," he says. "I'm sorry."

All I can say is, "You're alive."

"Who the hell's this?" Keith asks.

I introduce Jace, explain how we met in the forest, and explain to Jace how Tammy saved me. In turn, he explains how the others were shot for fighting or running, but they took him without question when he surrendered.

I describe Molly and Trish to Jace, but there are too many people here for him to know for sure if he's seen them. I even take a chance and mention the woman and her son from the house in East Elk, but of course, no luck. I don't even have names for them.

"If you saw them on the trucks, they're bound to be here," Jace says.

I just hope he's right. I've seen how trigger-happy some of these people can get, and it makes me sick.

"Back to the guards," Jace says. "We can't just sit around and wait. We need to do something."

"We are going to do something," Tammy chimes in.

"Look at them. There's a whole group of us here plotting away, and they don't even care. If we could get a few of the others, we could spread the word." Jace nods in the direction of the guards.

"And what do we do then? When everyone's yelling at the guards, getting them riled up, then what?" Keith argues, not liking where this conversation is headed.

Tammy shrugs. "Then we do what a mob does best. We overtake them, get the guns, and push our way out of this place." It's clear she and Jace are on the same page. I wonder why he's so adamant to fight now when back in the forest, he was so hesitant. Maybe it was seeing all his people shot and killed in front of his eyes.

"You're not worried about people dying in the process?" Keith asks, eyes darting between the two of them.

"Of course I am," Tammy answers. "But what else are we supposed to do? We came here for a reason."

"We were kidnapped!"

"We were going to sneak in anyway."

Keith shakes his head. "There has to be a better way."

Jace turns to me. "Ben? Are you in?"

It's been five days since this started. It can't go on much longer. It *won't* go on much longer. Either we hang on and don't get ourselves killed, banking on the FBI or some other organization saving us, or we do something that might get us killed.

Option two sounds risky and stupid, but there's something about doing nothing that makes my blood boil. Waiting like sheep in a slaughterhouse, thinking everything's going to work out just fine, might not work out as well as one might think.

Maybe it will...but like Keith said before—what happens when they decide it's time to send a message? I'm with my family now, they're safe and alive, and we're together. I'll be damned if I watch one of them be taken from me so that these people can prove a point to get their ransom money or whatever the hell they want.

"I'll do what I need to do," I say.

My wife squeezes my hand, her eyes shining with unshed tears as she nods her approval.

"But I think we need to make it clear to everyone involved that there's a very real risk either way."

"You've got to be kidding," Keith cries a little too loudly. "We have no guns, no weapons, no way to defend ourselves other than our literal fists. When we had the guns, that was one thing. But now—we have a better chance trying to sneak out under the cover of darkness than taking these assholes on face to face."

"Even if that's true, we're stronger as a united group," Jace says.

I turn to Rachel and the kids. "Maybe Keith is right. What should we do?"

"I think they're all right," Rachel says. "We need to do

something, and yes, it's dangerous. We spread the word that we're going to fight while at the same time doing as Keith suggested. If we can get the kids and some of the older folks out of here, give them a head start and safety from what's about to happen, it might be for the best."

"I can't leave you, Mom," Bea says, tucking her head into Rachel's shirt.

"I'll take care of you, Bea," Ryan says, wrapping his arms around his little sister.

The brimming tears in Rachel's eyes spill over. She wipes her face, smiling at our two brave kids. "You will be so much safer out there, loves. And you remember Keith, right? He's going with you. He'll protect you."

"I—" Keith startles but then nods. "That's right. I'm going with you."

"Good. We have a plan," Tammy says. "It's not long before dark. We better get moving."

Jace is the first to move. Tammy waits a few minutes before leaving, and Keith follows suit, leaving me alone with my family.

"It feels like it's been a year since I held you," I whisper in Rachel's ear.

She shivers. "I almost lost you, and I still might yet."

"You're not going to lose me. We're going to be fine. All of us."

Her eyes meet mine. She nods. "Let's get our babies out of here."

TWENTY-FIVE

As night falls, I sit huddled together with my wife and kids, mentally preparing for what's to come. Outside the barbed wire, the forest is creepy, and I wonder if there are eyes out there that belong to more than just animals. Of course there are. They've probably got satellites, night vision, inferred, and every other kind of sensor pointed right at us. The thought makes me feel a little better—a little less alone.

Maybe all they need is an opening. If people get out and away, is there going to be someone there waiting? I want to say *yes, of course*, but I'm not so sure.

There's been no one this whole time, no one in either East Elk or Welldeer. Why would they be out there now? No, I think they're there in another way, not physically, but through whatever technology permits.

How long will they spend negotiating? Five days is five too many for me, but I can see how it would all depend on the situation.

What do these people want? Tammy suggested a

ransom, but no one has flat-out said what they want or made any demands on us, other than simply being here and being compliant. What if they want something else, something far more sinister than just money? If it was just that, why would they go through all this trouble? Unless they want an ass load of it...but I think this is more than just a ransom at this point. This is an act of terror.

The word possesses a terrible power; just *thinking* it, panic swells in my bones, radiating through my body until I can feel it seep from my very pores. What would they be willing to do? Their aim might be totally different than any of us could even guess.

After asking countless people and attempting to call out their names before being silenced, I still haven't found Molly or Trish. As far as I can tell, they're not here, and that scares me most. What happened to them? I saw them get on that truck with my own eyes—

"Hey, you guys ready? It's about time," Keith whispers next to us. He's been fidgeting for the last hour, watching, and waiting for the darkness to envelop us just enough.

I hold my kids each a little tighter. "Protect each other," I say, giving them each a kiss on the forehead.

"We'll be okay, Dad," Ryan says.

Bea gives a soft sob into my chest. "I love you, Daddy."

"I love you both."

Rachel says her quick goodbyes to them, trying not to make it obvious to the guards. She and I both shake Keith's hand, then the three of them are off to join the others. We watch helplessly as he navigates into the shadows, out of sight. Others slink into the shadows a little at a time, remaining as inconspicuous as possible.

Rachel, I, and nearly everyone else watch the guards closer now than ever to see if they'll notice anything. Will they notice a few fewer bodies in their sleeping bags or a few fewer in the dirt? There are so many of us here. Is it really going to make a difference to them? We're hoping not, especially in the middle of the night. We're hoping our loved ones will slip beneath that barbed wire and be far away from this place by the time we need to act.

There are no lights for us to see. The guards wear night vision goggles, and we're left in the black forest, wondering if our loved ones have made it. Thirty minutes pass before we hear scuffling. Rachel sits up straighter, tilting her head to listen while others do the same.

Moments later, a scream—it's stifled quickly before another comes, and it, too, is cut off.

I turn toward my wife, barely able to see her wide, knowing eyes. She turns toward me. "Something's wrong, Ben."

Silent murmurs spread. Whispers of "Should we act now?"

"What should we do?" and "We need to do something" go around.

Followed by, "They need more time."

"It's too soon."

"Don't panic."

It only took an instant for our little plan to go right out the window, and it's too late now to do anything, even if we did ban together and follow through. A floodlight turns on, shining at our eyes. Laughter, so cold and calculating, comes from behind the light so we can't see who it is.

"You idiots," a voice says. "Did you really think that would work? And seriously—no one warned these instigators what happened to the first people who tried to slink away in the night?"

The first people? No one said anything about any others getting out. How could I have not thought of it? Of course they would've tried before now.

"Where are our kids?" Rachel screams at the voice, shielding her eyes from the blinding light.

"Lower the light a little, please," the voice says.

The spotlight dims slightly and angles upward. Shelly stands beside Keith and our kids, along with all the others who are held at gunpoint behind them.

Shelly—Keith—our neighbors are fucking in on this?

"You son of a bitch," I yell, looking Keith dead in his face.

He looks somewhat ashamed but remains standing next to his wife.

Shelly calls out, "Let's teach these people a much-needed lesson."

The guards open fire.

Rachel's screams are louder than the guns as she fights to get to our kids. It takes all my power and then some to hold her back, and I do it because it's not the kids they're firing on. It's us.

Others drop like flies as they're mowed down trying to

run. Even those who duck and cover as best they can are hit. A few bursts of bullets is all it takes to subdue us into submission—it's written all over the smug look on Shelly's face. She waves a hand for the guns to stop.

People lie injured, bleeding, and more terrified now than ever. It's exactly what she wanted.

"If you think we need to keep you alive, you're wrong," she says. "You're here because we need some of you in order to get what we want, not all. Not even close." She starts to pace. "So, keep it up if you want to. Keep seeing what kind of idiotic ideas you can come up with, and in the meantime, I'll keep those who are most...*vulnerable* in my safekeeping."

Cries go out instantly. Pleas for mercy, for reconsideration, for Shelly and the others to understand, along with demands that this is unethical and illegal, and they can't possibly do this. Someone calls, "Now! We have to act now!" And several people rise again to fight. I feel Rachel struggle in my arms again, but I hold her steady.

"That *bitch,* Ben!" she cries.

"Now's not the time," I whisper.

Shelly nods to the guards, who turn the lights back off, leaving us once again beneath a sheet of black. "You all can advance if you want to," she says.

Those who are ready to fight, hesitate. Despite what Shelly says, they're fully aware of the risk; they're not stupid. The difference is, as stupid as the idea might be, they're willing to do something about it because those are people they love over there.

Tammy must be among them because I hear her voice call, "They want a bloodbath. Well, we're not going to give it to them any more than they've already got."

"How can we trust them not to open fire whether we fight or not? Look what happened five minutes ago?" someone calls.

As we all consider the words, Shelly answers, "You can't." She laughs. "Sweet dreams, everyone."

TWENTY-SIX

The longest night of my life passes in a blur. Whispers and hisses come from all around me as people panic, but I can't get away from the ones in my head—the ones telling me what a failure I am. There are other, darker ones that have their say every now and then too, and those are the ones slowly driving me crazy.

They've divided us into two groups—one of us is expendable. Which one is it? And how long before they're done playing with us like a cat who's caught a mouse in its paws?

Either way, my children are over there. My wife over here. How can I protect them all when we're separated? How is Rach ever going to forgive me? Even if we make it out in one piece, how is she ever going to look at me the same? How will I look at myself?

When the hell is someone going to do something about this? Should we try again? How can we not? But the consequences if we fail again—

We didn't fail, though. Not really, did we? Because we

didn't try in the first place. We were cowards who stood by while they opened fire on us and held our families at gunpoint. What kind of people are we?

As disgusted as I am with myself for not saving my kids, for not getting my family out of this hellhole, as much as I *hate* it, I think it maybe means we're just normal. It's normal to not want to die, to not want to do anything that you know will cause you harm—a natural human instinct.

Our captors know it, and they're playing off our fear. Shelly knows it, and Keith—

Our neighbors.

As if reading my mind, Rachel speaks, pulling me from my demons. "We've known them for years. We trusted them, trusted Keith with our babies' lives, Ben!"

"I know."

"How could we not see it?"

I expect her to cry again, but she doesn't. Instead, she's a ball of rage, more furious than I've ever seen. I want to comfort her, but I don't know how; I don't even know how to comfort myself. And why should we feel comforted when our kids are over there with guns pointed at them? Any minute Shelly could have them shoot—

"We're going to figure this out," is all I can say.

"How? How can we possibly figure this out? Look what happened!" Rachel points to the people who were shot and killed, now lying to the side of the group. Those who were shot and injured were forced to find whatever they could to stop their bleeding, and some resulted in borrowing clean clothes from other victims who didn't make it.

Many people huddle together weeping, trying to seek comfort in each other as best they can, while others continue plotting. There's a third group, larger than either of the other two, just like Rachel and I, who are torn. We're frightened and angry and lost beyond words. We don't want to play with fire, but we also think that might be the only way, if done just right.

"I'm not an expert, Rach. I'm a goddamned analyst. You know that." She starts to pull away from me, but I hold on to her arm, wanting to make her listen. "What does an analyst do?"

She glares at me, rolls her eyes, and says, "An analyst analyzes."

"That's what I always say, and dammit, it's true. I'm going to analyze the shit out of these assholes, and we're going to think of something. But we can't play into what they want."

"Why didn't you analyze the shit out of Keith before we handed our children to him?" Rachel seethes.

"I—we both trusted him."

"Why did we trust him? Because he was our neighbor? We barely knew the man at all!" Her voice grows louder the angrier she becomes, and it's far from a whisper now. I want to tell her to calm down, but I know those two little words will get my head chewed off faster than anything else I could say.

"You're right. I should have paid more attention. I shouldn't have blindly handed our kids over. I'm sorry."

Her tears come now, bursting past the dam she built up. Rachel sobs into my shoulder while I do my best not to choke on my own. "I'm sorry," she says after a while, wiping her face.

When she calms, I finally offer the apology I should've given days ago. "I'm sorry about that morning —with the suit. It was so stupid. I was an ass."

She nods through her tears. "Yeah, you were. But it's okay. Do you want to talk about how the meeting went?"

"No. But you know what?"

"What?"

"After this, I think I'm going to find a new job."

"That bad, huh?"

"It's not just the meeting. It's…" I release a deep breath. "It's every day, and I know I can do better."

Rachel nods. "Good for you."

Dawn inches its way up the horizon as I hold her. Nothing I say will be good enough—not for her, for me, so I remain silent, feeling her chest rise and fall as her breathing slows back to normal. When she's calm again, I take her hand, and keeping low so we're not targets, we make our way toward Tammy.

TWENTY-SEVEN

At least with daylight, we have a visual on our kids again. It's the one good thing I can focus on as hunger, thirst, fear, and anger threaten to overwhelm me. The guards keep us from calling out to them, but at least we can see them. They're close and they're as okay as they can be.

"I have some good news for everyone," Shelly greets us with a broad grin. "We worked out a deal, and you'll be able to check out of Hotel California really soon. We just need a little more cooperation, and we'll hand you over to the nice federal agents, safe and sound."

A few people scoff their disbelief, daring to call out, "They'll never let you live, you psycho terrorist bitch!"

Shelly's eyes flash. "Whoever said that, feel free to come forward and say it to my face."

Silence.

"Oh, come on. Don't be shy. I promise not to bite." She waits a few moments before continuing. "I could've made things a hell of a lot worse for you. Just remember that." A helicopter flies overhead as if to cement Shelly's words into us. She's not lying. This is finally going to be over soon.

Shelly beams at us. "I really should be thanking you. Without that display last night, we'd still be standing in quicksand with our negotiators. It seems that was just the kick in the ass they needed."

She splays her hands wide in a gesture of innocence. "We're going to release some of the most vulnerable first to show our good faith before we get what we want." She claps her hands as if it's time to celebrate, and a few people actually clap with her. Hell, I almost want to, too. I wonder if she knows who insulted her and if she secretly has her eye on them. I wouldn't be surprised if she did and if, somehow, they didn't make it out of here, despite her claims of *working a deal*.

I'm sure that deal doesn't involve killing any more people, either, but something inside tells me we haven't seen the end of Shelly's rage. From what I've learned during the time she was our neighbor, although it could've been an act all along, patience doesn't seem like her strong suit. And when someone does something she doesn't like or *insults* her—she gets her payback.

"What do you want?" someone else dares call to her.

Shelly tilts her head, turning to Keith and a few of her guards. "What do you say, guys? What do we want?"

"What does anyone want?" one of the guards says.

"Money, amnesty, new identity, new lives," Keith says.

"You had a good goddamned life!" Rachel calls. She holds the side of my shirt in a death-grip, digging her nails into what's left of the fabric, as if willing me to hold her back.

"You don't know anything—" Keith starts before Shelly cuts him off.

"There you have it. We answered your question. Now be good little sheep and obey mama. The handoff is in twenty minutes. Anyone does anything to fuck this up, you're going to regret it; mark my words."

Shelly walks through the group, selecting five individuals to let go.

Don't do it, Shelly, don't you fucking do it!

Her eyes land on Ryan and Bea, who haven't let go of each other since last night. It doesn't even take a split second for her to decide. She reaches a hand out to grip Bea's little arm. Ryan holds onto his sister, too far away for me to hear the words between them. He struggles to hold on, to protect Bea, and keep from separating at all costs.

Shelly reaches back to slap Ryan, leaving a bright red handprint across his face. I'm not sure whose scream is louder—Bea's, Rachel's, or mine. Rachel is murderous, screaming and yelling, and the guards move to block her while Ryan and Bea continue to struggle. Finally, Shelly pulls out a pistol and holds it in front of Ryan.

Rachel howls.

I can see the fear in my son's eyes as he scans for me.

This is going to haunt him forever. And for that, no matter what happens, I want that bitch to pay. For everything—the murders, the kidnapping, the terror, yes—but more than anything, for robbing my children of their innocence.

Ryan's eyes land on mine. I nod, and I know he can't hear me, not with the screaming and everything else, so I mouth, *It's okay, son. Let go.*

He looks down at his little sister, his tears visible from even this distance, and—a shot rings out.

My heart stops.

Rachel chokes beside me, a silent scream on her lips as she hyperventilates.

My ears ring as the entire world seems to go silent. Still.

Shelly drops. Dead.

The guards are in a frenzy, running and yelling and trying to figure out what the hell is going on. Was it a sniper that shot her? Was it one of us? And if so, who the hell has the gun?

Tammy's voice rings above all others. "Now! We need to RUN!"

This time, there's no doubt. We need to take advantage while the shit has hit the fan. The guards are a disorganized mess, and we're not going to sit here like ducks and make it easy for them.

I hold Rachel's hand as I half hobble-run, trying to weave a path to our kids without falling. More shots ring out, but we keep going until they're within reach. Rachel clings to both of them, crying, "I'm never letting go of either of you again!"

"Come on, guys," I say, leading them all toward the barbed wire. I've lost sight of Tammy and Jace but spot them again when I see where everyone's headed.

Shit.

"There are too many of us all in one spot. Come on, this way." I lead my family in a different direction so we might be less conspicuous with the guards' attention on the bigger group.

Rachel and I take hold of the wire and help Bea

through first, followed by Ryan. They stand on the other side as Rachel climbs through next, and finally me. The sense of freedom fills my veins and my lungs, the air sweeter somehow.

We try to keep low and out of sight as shots continue to ring out. The guards are still hunting people down, and many who are trying to get through can't. When I glance back to see, it appears they're regaining their hold on things, and those who were in the back of the group were never able to make it out.

We would've been back there too.

I grip Rachel's hand a little tighter. We're on the road from hell, and we're not out of the woods yet.

She opens her mouth to say something—but the sound of engines starting fills the air. Her face drains of color. "Ben—"

"They're starting the trucks. We have to run now."

"But your leg, Ben!"

I turn to my kids, looking them each dead in the eyes. "You keep going, no matter what. If I can't keep up if something happens. You don't stop. Not until you see the police. You got it?"

They both nod.

"Good. And don't let go of each other. I'm proud of you both."

I take the lead, knowing that even though they say they won't, they'll slow their pace to keep with me. How could they not? I need to show them I can make it, at least until we get a little farther, so I grit my teeth against the pain, and I go.

TWENTY-EIGHT

It feels like I'm stuck in a time loop, doomed to run through the forest for eternity, except this time, I have my family with me. Without the cover of darkness, we're open targets for those hunting us. The only cover we have is the trees themselves, and hope that separating from the others helps make us less noticeable.

The trucks sound in the distance, seeming to travel the opposite direction as us. For now. I cringe as we hear screams from those recaptured. It also seems they're keeping the shooting to a minimum, and I wonder if that's because they're so low on hostages now.

Where the hell is the cavalry? Now would be the perfect time to swoop in and save the day. What the hell are they waiting for?

"Did you see how many were still left behind?" Rachel asks.

"No," I pant. "But it looked like a lot made it out."

She shakes her head. "Ben, there were tons still left

"I don't know. I just saw them," she snaps. We've slowed again for us all to catch our breath. My lungs burn as I wheeze in gulps of oxygen. The kids look in good shape, but it's obvious they need water.

I think about the river and waterfall from the other day. Seems like I was there five minutes ago. The gurgling rocks beneath the surface, the fish swimming beneath the clear surface... my mouth goes drier, if it's even possible.

"There's a river somewhere around here."

"How do you know?" She throws my words back at me, clearly annoyed.

I try to form enough spit inside my mouth to coat my throat and tongue before speaking. "I just know." I smile, trying to relay I'm joking, but Rachel only glares.

"Okay, where is it?"

"Not sure."

"Well, that's a big help!"

"We need water, Rach. I know it's here—" I stop, remembering how far it was from East Elk and how we're nowhere near it now. Sure, there's a river—but we're never going to reach it. Not today.

I listen. The trucks are still out there, but not as far now. "Are they headed toward us?" I whisper.

We listen again, all four sets of ears straining to determine which direction they're heading.

"We need to hide," Rachel whispers.

Tammy, where are you and that gun when I need you? It's the first thought that pops into my head when she mentions hiding. Tammy saved my ass when I was tucked inside that tree. If it happens again, I don't know if we'll be so lucky a second time.

"There's nowhere to hide. We keep moving for now." I swoop Bea up onto my back and she hangs on tight as we pick up the pace again. Internally, I will my heart and lungs not to burst as I push myself past my limits.

"Where are we going, Ben? We can't keep blindly running through the forest. We need to get our bearings," Rachel says.

"Our bearings are to get as far away from those trucks as we can."

"And in the meantime, we're lost and wind up starving to death."

"We're not lost." She might be right, but I'll never admit it because I'm right too. The only thing that matters at this exact moment is making sure we're in the clear, away from those people, and not going to get taken again.

"And what happens when we wind up running in circles and end up right back on their front doorstep?" Rachel stops. Before I know what she's doing, she sucks in a deep breath and screams, "Help!"

"What are you doing?" I hiss.

She ignores me, calling out again, "Help! Over here!"

I reach for her, to do what, I don't know—either cover her mouth or shake her, but she backs away from me. The kids are watching us, wide-eyed, unsure what's going on between us, and the sight kills me. "Rachel, stop," I beg, but she only yells again and again.

It feels like the world is closing in on us, the trees looming down over our heads, squeezing in tighter. Is it me, or is there suddenly less oxygen in the atmosphere? I can't leave them. I won't. But Rachel is going to get us all killed if she keeps yelling.

"Rach—the trucks."

She finally meets my gaze. "That's not all I hear, Ben."

I listen again, hope blooming at the look on her face. There—someone is calling back to us. Rachel beams at me before leading the way toward the voices.

W e hurry, sure we can't be the only ones who heard. The trucks could easily be on us any minute they decide to head this way. My knee gives out once, sending me sprawling, but Rachel is by my side to support me before I fall. Despite our rush, she slows our pace without comment.

The kids are in front of us, within arm's reach. Ryan points ahead. "I see smoke."

"Not much farther, Rachel says, urging us on."

But there's something about the smoke that I don't like. Something is just not right. Why would there be smoke? "Wait—" I start.

"It's okay, we'll be with the others in a minute. Look how close we are," Rachel says.

"No, hang on." I pull away from her. "Everyone stop. There's something wrong."

The kids listen on bated breath, but my wife is only

frustrated with me again. She's anxious to get to the others, believes there's safety in numbers, that one of them is bound to have a gun if the one who shot Shelly is there—or at the very least, they'll have a plan figured out. She just doesn't understand—

Leaves crunch as someone approaches. Rachel and I pull the kids in close. With no time to do anything else, we wait, holding on to each other.

Tammy and Jace step out. "Good god, we've been looking everywhere for you," Tammy cries.

It's so good to see her I could kiss her. She gives Rachel and me each a hug while Jace gives a handshake. "There are so many others scattered through here. We didn't know if we'd find you or someone else," Jace says.

"We thought that was your smoke signal over there," Rachel says, pointing to the faint, white plume through the trees.

Tammy turns to me, drained of all color. She shakes her head. "We need to run, Ben."

"Damn, here I was, hoping you would stick around a while," a voice says.

We turn as one to see a familiar, sinister face.

"Have we met before?" he asks, tilting his head. "Ah, that's right. You're the one that got away. Don't worry. I don't make the same mistake twice."

The armed men who pulled me from the hunting cabin my first night in the forest are here again. It's their campfire smoke in the distance—and we walked right into their laps.

TWENTY-NINE

No, no, no! This can't be happening again! First the car wreck, then the forest, now this—what's next?

Holding Bea's hand, Ryan takes off at a sprint. The man in charge barks a few orders, and as a few others branch off to chase after them, he calls, "You wouldn't want your parents to die, kids, would you?"

"Bastard," Rachel says.

The man only shrugs. "You've got five seconds to get your asses back over here before I put a hole in your mom's dirty mouth." He and some others point guns at the rest of us. "If anyone says a single word, I'll blow all your fucking heads off."

There's nothing any of us can do. We're unarmed and vulnerable—completely at their mercy as Ryan is forced to make another life-altering decision. *Keep running*, I silently plead. *Keep going. Don't stop.*

Whether these people follow through on their threat or not, I don't want my kids here, and without her saying so, I know Rachel feels the same. They need to get as far away as they can, and with every fiber of my being, I hope Ryan remembers my words. *Keep running no matter what happens.*

I hold my wife's hand, squeezing it as tightly as I dare as we watch our son continue to pull our daughter through the forest. Bea struggles in his grip, looking back with wide tearful eyes, seeing her parents in the worst possible situation. Ryan doesn't look back, though. He keeps his face straight ahead, pulling her with.

They weave between the trees, faster, more agile than the men chasing them. Pride swells in my chest watching them. Our boy's a runner, alright. He can run circles around almost anyone and can sure as hell outrun the shit out of these people. *They're going to be okay.*

My eyes shift to meet Rachel's, her own emotions mirroring mine. Her lips turn upward into a barely perceptible smile as if to say, good for him. Then her lips cave inward as a bullet punches a hole right through.

Her eyes bulge at the initial shock as blood and brain matter spray from her face. My jaw drops in a silent scream. I pull her close, unable to breathe, incapable of registering what's happening.

Rachel's lifeless body collapses into me. I rock her back and forth, my gentle attempts to wake her growing more frantic by the second. Her blood smears into my skin and clothes, but I don't notice until she's ripped from me and tossed to the ground.

The scream finally escapes my lips, a desperate, raging roar. The edge of a barrel is placed against my forehead. "Go ahead. Do something," the unnamed man says without a care in the world.

My eyes dart toward Ryan, who's now too far out of

sight. I don't know if they stopped running or if they saw their mother's face implode. "Don't you fucking stop!" I yell at the top of my lungs, my vocal cords straining.

"You know, there's something about you that I just don't like." The unnamed man growls.

He's going to shoot. He's going to end me just like he did to Rachel. My eyes move from the forest, where I can no longer see my son, to Tammy. I haven't seen her cry like this before. We've been through a lot in such a short amount of time, but she's been a warrior through everything, taking even the worst of the blows in stride. Now, she looks broken, defeated. Her expression resembles almost a sliver of the black mass swelling inside me.

The unnamed man reaches back.

I brace myself to die.

But he doesn't shoot. Instead, he pistol whips the side of my face. I fall to my knees, and once I'm down, he kicks, bringing his steel toe boot against my already broken body. Tammy and Jace's screams are distant, faint sounds in an echo chamber of ringing madness.

Part of me welcomes the beating because the physical pain is a start to drown out the emotional. I need it to take away the image of my wife's face, stained into my memory for eternity. *Keep running, Ryan, and don't let go of Bea for anything.*

I lose consciousness, for how long, I'm not sure. When I'm lucid again, there's a shift in the atmosphere. Static plays from a walkie-talkie, followed by rapid voices.

Rough hands grip me and pull. I'm dragged across the forest floor, pulling leaves and brambles in my wake. There's no mercy shown, only an insistent, relentless, dragging until my skin swells beneath the heat of a campfire.

Black pulses at the edge of my vision, and I struggle to keep my eyes open. I watch as Jace avoids being shot to fight tooth and nail to get a gun. Then he is shot, but he keeps fighting, while Tammy is already bound with rope, wriggling to get free.

Jace gets hold of the gun, gets off one shot, two—

One of the others drop.

There's another shot, and Jace drops next.

Tammy chokes beneath her gag as he tries to crawl back toward her feet before falling limp.

"Enough!" a voice calls. Keith and a few more armed guards approach. "I leave you alone for five minutes, and it's a bloodbath," he says, addressing my wife's murderer. Keith looks around us, his eyes finally landing on me. He winces. "I asked you not to kill him."

The unnamed man holds his hands out. "He's alive."

Keith frowns. "And the woman?"

"You didn't say anything about her."

"I take it she didn't make it, then?"

"You take it right."

Keith's frown deepens, but he nods. "Look, we have bigger problems on our plate. We need to talk." He places a hand on the man's arm and leads him away, where he thinks Tammy and I can't hear, but it's not far enough. I'm not able to catch everything, but a few words get through.

"Shelly...taken care of," Keith says.

"Others?"

"Looking...plan is still...."

"Hold it—" the unnamed man barks.

The whole world goes silent again, and I'm not sure if I've blacked out again. After a moment I hear his arms making rapid gestures toward the others in silent instruction. A heartbeat later, I hear something else. Trucks.

The trucks are here. They finally found us. Where will we go now? Does it matter? But...why would they be worried about the trucks if the people in the trucks are working with them?

Hands wrap around my wrists again, this time pulling me up to my feet. An involuntary groan escapes as the pain radiates from my bones. Keith asks, "Where're the kids, Ben?" As he pulls me away from the fire.

"Fuck you," I spit.

"Fair enough." He pauses. "I'm sorry about Rachel."

"Don't you dare." I shift in his grip, throwing us both off balance. Keith lets go as I fumble to stay on my feet.

"Don't fight me goddammit, Ben. I may be a part of this, but I still like you."

"You *like* me? You lured me here!"

"I had to, don't you see?"

"The car chase? You had to do that too, right?"

"That was all Shelly. I thought it was real until I recognized our men. She never told me." He reaches for my arm again, but I avoid him in a clumsy attempt to dodge.

"Stay away from me, Keith."

"Do you want to be beaten again? You're my hostage until I say otherwise," he growls, pulling a handgun from his side holster. "We may have been friendly at one point. But you will not disrespect me in front of my people."

"You killed your own wife, then you allowed them to kill mine," I say.

He works his jaw but doesn't deny the accusation. "Come on. We're getting the hell out of here before they get to us."

"Who—"

"Just shut up and move, Ben!" He half pushes, half drags me forward.

"There a problem here, boss?" one of the other unnamed asks.

"*Is* there a problem, Ben?" Keith asks, glaring at me.

Watching as Tammy is led away ahead of me, I shake my head *no*.

"Good," Keith says. "Let's move."

THIRTY

The familiar white trucks are waiting for us. I could swear one of them is the same that's had its tire blown out by us a few times. *There's no way Keith didn't recognize it.*

"You were so damned convincing," I say under my breath, thinking of the car chase. No wonder he knew exactly where to go. *I should've suspected something was wrong.*

Keith is close enough to hear but doesn't respond. Instead, he leads me around to the tailgate. I don't know how the hell he thinks I'm going to pull myself up in there. I can barely walk as it is. Two others come around to help push me up. It's a struggle for all of us, but eventually they roll me up and inside.

"Hurry up, they're almost here!" Keith cries. The trucks are almost on us now, and I wonder again why he's so afraid of them if they're working together. Unless they know he shot Shelly, and he knows they'll kill him for it.

Panting, groaning, desperately hanging on to

consciousness, I feel Tammy's grip on my shoulder. "Hang on, Ben," she whispers.

The tailgate slams shut, and just as everyone shuffles away to load up, a voice echoes through a loudspeaker. "This is the FBI. We have you surrounded."

The lightbulb goes off when I finally see the trucks we've been running from pull through the foliage and emerge in a wide arc around us. The trucks full of people we thought were out to get us, were hunting us—are the FBI. Here to save us from this hell.

And we ran.

Where the hell are my kids?

The tension is palpable as those who are armed argue about the next move. Immediately, Keith returns to the tailgate, pointing a gun at Tammy and me. "We have hostages!" he cries.

The rest back themselves into a protective perimeter around the truck.

A helicopter flies overhead so low it looks like some of the trees might fall from the wind it's producing.

My wife's murderer joins us, with a gun now to Tammy's head, as if he needs to make the hostage point more evident.

"It's over," the voice says through the loudspeaker. "Let the hostages go. We can resolve this peacefully."

"Like hell we can," Keith calls back. "Let us the hell out of here, then we can come to a peaceful conclusion."

What's he going to do when he realizes there's no more out for him? What's this other asshole going to do to Tammy when he realizes it? There won't be any more ordering him or telling him what to do.

"Why don't you tell them you want to talk," I say. "See if they'll meet you in the middle."

I can feel his calculation as he narrows his eyes at me. He turns to the unnamed man holding Tammy to ask, "What do you think?"

For a heartbeat, as his attention is drawn to Keith, his grip on the gun falters. The gun tilts just a few inches from her head, and from the corner of my eye, I see Tammy reaching for something.

My throat closes up as my brain cries out, *No, Tammy! Don't!*

But she's not going for his gun. She's going for her own. Before my eyes can register her movements, she pulls the gun and shoots the unnamed man in the temple. Point blank. Dead.

Keith staggers back as if to distance himself from her, but she pulls the trigger again, without hesitation, killing him in a single shot.

The others turn toward us, rifles raised to shoot, but before they can open fire, agents move in. "Get down!" Tammy cries, shoving me back down on the truck bed.

Bullets rain over us as the armed captors—murderers—refuse to go down without a fight. They take cover behind the truck, still trying to use us any way they can. A few attempt to climb up inside the tailgate with us, but Tammy quickly puts an end to that before it can start.

I lay, staring at her, not knowing what the hell to think, but also thinking not for the first time, how damned lucky I am she found me.

Tammy gives a small smile.

"You're the one who killed Shelly. It wasn't Keith."

She nods. "That bitch deserved it, Ben, and then some."

"How'd you keep the gun? How'd you—" Wait. "You had it this whole time." She could have saved Rachel. She could have done something.

There's no time for her to answer. Another stray bullet pings off the interior of the tailgate, ricocheting, narrowly missing us. There's nothing else for us to use for protection besides the truck itself.

When she has an opening, Tammy crawls toward the back window of the truck, tests it, and when it slides open, she wedges herself through. Moments later, the engine starts. Those who are hiding behind the tires, cry out, and desperate for their lives, they renew their efforts to pull themselves up inside with me.

I kick at fingers and hands, claw at faces, scream and spit, and fight any way I can as the bastards keep coming. Like a hoard of zombies that won't fucking die, they keep coming, until finally, Tammy pulls away. The rear tires spit dirt as they struggle to gain traction. When she takes off, she only drives a few yards before stopping again. "Stay down, Ben!" she calls through the still-open window.

She doesn't have to tell me twice. I'm frozen in place, listening to the sounds of that long-awaited calvary come riding in. A few more shots go off, but for the most part, it's all over. Calls go around as officers communicate in their jargon, make arrests, and call for a second airlift.

Tammy calls from the window, "Agent Tammy Souza." She holds a badge out the window, and once she gets the go-ahead to step out, relays the pertinent information to other officers as the area is swept for stragglers.

Meanwhile, I feel like an afterthought. *Good.* I want to be left alone now. *I just want my kids.*

As the adrenaline seeps back out of my system, I'm pulled down, down, down. The black has returned to the corners of my vision. Everyone's voices around me sound muted and loud at the same time. I'm so sleepy. If I fall asleep, will they let me stay that way? Or will some asshole come and wake me up?

Before I have the chance to find out, Tammy is back, a familiar hand on my shoulder, her voice calling instructions. Almost directly overhead, something is coming toward me from the sky. I start to jerk away, but Tammy holds me still.

"Shh," she says. "We're going to get you to the hospital now, Ben. It's over."

THIRTY-ONE

I don't have to open my eyes to know I'm in a hospital bed. The heart rate monitor beeps in my ear in a slow and steady rhythm. Gradually, I become aware of my body, the aches and pains, both deep in my bones and higher on the surface of my skin, stretched tight with stitches.

An IV drip connects to my vein, along with whatever cocktail of painkillers they're putting in me. I don't have to see them to know they're there or feel the haze they induce.

My wife is dead.

There's no drug in the world that can take that away. I don't want to open my eyes, to *exist* without her here.

Flashes of her death replay over and over—the way her lips caved inward in a horrible backward grin, the way she dropped, lifeless without a second thought. Her eyes. *She didn't even know what hit her.* And I just stood there.

Just like I stood there, watching Jack get beaten by the campfire, then watching his head get blown off while lying in a heap of rubble, watching Molly and Trish leave that house—the woman and her boy too. Just like I let my boss walk all over me at work because I was so desperate to make a good impression. For what? I just stood by and let these things happen. It feels like that's the story of my life—Ben, the guy who stood by and watched while shit hit the fan and sprayed everyone in the face.

I'm never going to just stand by and let something happen again. Never.

What the hell am I going to do now?

I feel like part of me died right alongside Rachel. I don't feel the same; I don't recognize my own body. Everything feels different, and I'm not sure it will ever go back. How could it? Without her, I wouldn't want it to anyway.

The sound of my daughter's voice draws me in. "Daddy?" She places her little hand on mine, rubbing her fingers into my skin.

"He's still sleeping," Ryan says. "Leave him be, Bea."

My boy. Of course he knows I'm not sleeping. It's impossible for him to miss my fist clenched around the sheet, the sound of my teeth grinding together, or the tears that slip down the side of my face.

Rachel is gone.

But my kids aren't. They're still here and they need me like never before. I saw it in her eyes as the life left her —my wife was *glad* to know they were together, protecting each other, putting each other above *anyone*, even her. That's what matters. And she'd expect me to do the same.

Our kids come first. No matter what.

I allow my eyes to flutter open. "I'm awake," I rasp.

They each lean down to hold me, and I hug them

back with all the strength left in me. "I'm so sorry about everything," I whisper.

"They told us about Mom," Ryan says. He wipes his face against my chest, refusing to look at me while he cries.

"I hope you didn't see."

He shakes his head. "No. We heard though." He sobs into me then. "Dad, we should've just come back. It's all my fault."

"I want you to look at me, son."

Ryan lifts his head, tears and snot streaming. He glares at me, full of shame that cuts me to my core.

"She wanted you to keep running. We both did. Don't you ever blame yourself; not even for a second. If you would've come back, it would've been you or your sister shot instead of Mom. There was nothing—nothing any of us could've done."

Tears flow from my own eyes, and I don't wipe them. I let him see my sincerity, hoping, praying that it'll get through to him. So much has been taken from him the last few days, and the last thing he needs is to live with guilt on his shoulders for the rest of his life. It's not his burden to bear.

"Dad, I have something else to tell you," Ryan whispers.

"What is it?"

He hides his face into my chest again before mumbling, "I took your suit."

I blink. *Did I just hear him right?* The suit, the argument, it feels like a lifetime ago. Why did it matter again? "I—what happened to it?" I ask.

Thinking about that suit—it's hard not to think about

it, but it seems like my entire story would've turned out differently without that goddamned thing. I wouldn't have spent so much time worrying about it, wouldn't have been late to work, wouldn't have believed I needed it in order to be successful, wouldn't have stayed late, wound up on that freeway...Rachel would've stayed home.

But it's not Ryan taking it that caused the collision course. It's *me*, my determination that I absolutely one hundred percent needed that object in order to succeed. If it wasn't the suit, it would've been something else. It was always going to be something.

I'm the one who could've just said *no* to working late, to putting up with all the shit that my boss put me through. I *chose* to stay late and probably would have even if I was on time, wearing my *power suit*, spic and span. In fact, if he hadn't taken it, I'm not sure if I really would've learned a lesson at all. I should be thanking him.

"I wanted to see what it felt like," Ryan says. "You just looked...happy, I guess, in it, and I wanted to see what it was like. But I ripped it while I was trying it on, and I thought you'd rip me a new one...so I hid it."

I smile a little, imagining the oversized suit swallowing his skinny body whole. I probably would've torn him a new one that morning. But that was then. Now, things are so different.

Instead of reprimanding him, I ask, "You're not happy?"

"I mean, yeah, I guess I am—well, I was...but not like that look you had when you had it on."

I grip his hand tighter. "That's called confidence, son. And it's the best. But you don't need a suit to find it."

"Your dad's right," a voice says.

The three of us look up to see Tammy in the doorway. Stepping into the room, looking at Ryan and Bea, she says, "I was there, remember? I saw what happened, and I want you to know you saved your sister's life. In so many ways. You are a hero, Ryan. You should be proud of yourself, not ashamed, and never guilty. And confidence—you should be so full of yourself that it makes your dad sick, because you're that bad ass."

Ryan flushes. "I don't think so, but thanks."

"Trust me, kid. Not everyone would've put their sister first the way you did. Over and over your lives were on the line. You're a good person and you should *believe* it. One day you'll figure it out, and when you do, you'll understand. For your sake, I hope it's sooner rather than later."

Ryan only nods. His color deepens when Bea leans to give him a kiss on the cheek. "Thank you," she says, wrapping her arms around his neck.

Smiling, Tammy looks at me next. "I just came to say goodbye and—" She clears her throat. "And that I'm sorry I wasn't able to say more or—do more. I was just doing my job as best I could." She shrugs.

"Did you know Keith was involved? At the house— you wanted him with us."

"Not him, no. But his wife, we suspected."

"I can't believe you didn't warn me, Tammy."

"It was need-to-know, unconfirmed information, Ben. I thought I had it under control—I'm sorry. There's so much I'd do differently if I could."

I pause before saying, "You got the bad guys in the end."

She smirks. "Yes, we did."

"And you saved my life. More than once."

"Like I said, doing my job."

"Doesn't matter if it was your job or not. You did it and I can't be mad at you for who you didn't save or what you didn't do. I want to be, but I can't. Thank you, Tammy—if that's your real name, for everything. For being there. If you weren't—I don't know how many of us would still be stuck in that camp." I give her a meaningful look, nodding toward the kids. I hope she understands. I owe her not only my life but my children's lives as well.

"Yes, Tammy's my real name. And you're welcome, Ben," she says, the flush in her face now matching Ryan's.

"Will you do me a favor?" I ask.

"Anything that's within my power."

"Is it within your power to find someone? I mean, I'm sure there are people looking for friends and family after all this, right?"

Tammy purses her lips in thought. "Are you talking about those women who helped you?"

"They saved my life. I let them—" I clear my throat. "I watched them get onto one of those trucks. I couldn't find them in the safe zone, Tammy. I just have to know if they're—if—"

"Well...is one of them named Molly?"

I sit up a little straighter, wincing as I do. "You found them."

Tammy smiles. "I wanted a minute with you to say goodbye before I let them in the room."

"Holy shit. They're here?"

"They found me first, believe it or not. And they wouldn't take no for an answer. They insisted on seeing that you were okay." She opens the door to welcome them in, and there they are—Molly and Trish. They're alive.

"I thought you were dead," I say.

Molly laughs. "We thought the same of you."

I turn to my kids. "You guys, this is Molly and Trish. They saved my life when I was trying to get home." I explain to them about being with Jack and the urgent care building collapsing, and the way these two ran into me.

"How'd you make it off the truck?" I ask.

"Well, we didn't," Trish starts.

"We tried to!" Molly laughs.

They share another one of their looks like they can read each other's mind with only a glance and a smile. It makes my heart hurt for Rachel because we were just like that. *And I took it for granted.*

Trish continues, "When they locked those doors, we obviously knew something was wrong. Everyone on the truck was freaking out, but we had time to talk to people, figure out if anyone had anything useful, all that jazz. Anyway, long story short, no one had jack shit, and we weren't able to get off the truck."

"Okay, so then what? You weren't at the safe zone when I was, were you? I tried to find you."

"When they pulled up to the safe zone, I'm talking like immediately, we snuck out with a few others while there was a commotion," Trish says. "I'm not sure they even noticed. And to answer your question, no—I'm pretty sure we weren't there when you were. At least, I don't think we were. We went up the road to Rock Creek."

"Son of a bitch."

"I know, right?"

"They tried to make everyone think that anyone who got out was gunned down."

Molly scoffs. "Of course they want people to think that. Would you expect anything else?"

I shake my head. "Nope, sure wouldn't." Fear is the best way to control people. "I'm just glad you're both alive."

They step closer to my bed, each resting a hand on my feet. "We're so sorry for what you went through, Ben," Trish says. Her eyes brim with tears and I have to look away.

"We *all* went through hell," I say.

"You can say that again," Molly says.

I look back to Tammy. "What's going to happen now? The roads are shit, people and families destroyed. No one can trust anyone at this point."

"That's going to be up to the towns and local governments to determine the logistics. But if you're referring to the people, not just the infrastructure, I think they'll do what they always do. They'll band together and support each other, hold each other up to get through the darkest times."

It's going to be chaos for a long time. Things like this don't just happen and go away, they change the world, whether for the better or worse. I pull my kids close to my chest again, breathing in their scents, taking strength from their freely given love. We're going to get through this together.

Something tells me Tammy's right to be optimistic. The world seems to have a way of balancing itself out. The scales may tip one way, may seem like everything is going to hell in a handbasket, but then they have a way of tipping themselves just right in the opposite direction to even themselves out. The inferno cools eventually, and just like she said, people will be there to pick each other up and brush off the ashes.

THANK YOU

Enjoyed Inferno Road?

Please consider leaving a review.

Reviews help authors more than you might think. Even just a few words make a difference and are greatly appreciated. The best place to review is whichever retailer you purchased from, but you can also consider Goodreads or BookBub.

BONUS
CHAPTER

Did you wonder what happened to Rachel when the call with Ben dropped at the beginning of the book? Or how she and the kids wound up where they did?

Sign up for my newsletter by going to:
https://BookHip.com/DFHQNCP
and I'll send you a bonus chapter from her point of view!

AUTHOR'S NOTE

The idea for this book came to me in 2015, when at the time I wanted to make a game for the app store. I had recently gotten an Apple watch, which was new technology then, and games and other applications were pretty limited. I was also really into learning about programming and application design, and I wanted to get some experience under my belt because I had virtually none.

My idea was to make a story-based game written in second person, where the player would be the character deciding the choices. In this case, there would've been no "Ben." The player would've been doing the actions and making the choices, similar to a "choose your path" type novel. That's when I first started outlining and jotting down bits of ideas for this story.

Needless to say, life happened, and the game didn't. Flash forward to 2021, when I was just getting started as a full-time author. I was going through some old files and came across the story—nameless at the time.

I thought what a shame to have it go to waste, especially because I felt there was some real potential. The story kept coming back to me from time to time, and I was excited to come across these long-lost files. So, I sat down and started working at it, with the new intention of turning it into a choose-your-path type book since that was the original kind of style I intended.

After some more research, it seemed like there wouldn't be much of an adult audience for a book like that, and most readers wanted an actual story, or at least that's what I decided at the time. The story, as it stood at this point, was about 5,000 words in the second person point of view and consisted of "choices" branching out in all different directions, many of them leading to death for the main character. At one point, I thought of calling the story *Bound for Death.*

I set the story aside for another time while the idea continued to sort of stew at the back of my mind. Finally, after writing eight books, as 2022 came to a close, I decided I was ready to tackle the project once and for all. I struggled a bit with which point of view I wanted to follow, starting with third-person, and ultimately rewriting into first-person—*Ben's* point of view.

I wanted to honor my original idea by keeping the player or *reader* in the sense that they were still in the driver's seat, and I think being inside that main character's head, in the here and now, was one of the best ways to accomplish it.

Of course, I made the story more complex, adding in all the supporting characters and the rest of the story, changing names, adding background, and all the important details that go into a novel. But the initial journey of this story started back in 2015 when I had the simple, innocent thought: "What if you were driving home from work and the freeway blew up?"

ACKNOWLEDGMENTS

I have a couple of amazing teammates who have been right by my side throughout this amazing journey. My husband and my son—having their full support, encouragement, understanding, and patience is priceless. Thank you both from the bottom of my heart.

To my editing team at My Brother's Editor, your hard work and consistency is exceptional. Thank you for being so amazing at what you do.

To Karen and Sara, thank you for being the first ones to read this book and for giving me vital feedback. Your help is invaluable and is so appreciated.

To Angie, thank you for helping me come up with an awesome title and blurb.

Also a special thank you to my father-in-law for the useful tidbit about using a car's headrest to break through a window.

To my faithful readers, you and your continued support are everything to me! Thank you for sticking with me, for encouraging me, fanning the flames, and for picking up each new book that releases.

And finally, thank you, dear reader, for showing me your support by reading this book. Whether you are new to my work or are one who keeps coming back for more, I truly hope you enjoyed the read.

ABOUT
K. LUCAS

K. Lucas is an author who lives for the unexpected twist. Originally from California, she now lives in the Pacific Northwest with her husband, son, dogs, cats, and chickens. After earning a bachelor's degree in information technology, she became a homeschool mom and then a full-time author. She loves all things thrilling & chilling, and her favorite pastimes include reading, watching scary movies, and exploring nature.

www.klucasauthor.com

CONNECT WITH
K. LUCAS

For text message notifications
text KLUCAS to 877-618-4214

Join the Facebook reader group
The Edge of Your Seat Club

Website:
www.klucasauthor.com

Newsletter:
www.klucasauthor.com/newslettersignup

amazon.com/author/klucas

goodreads.com/klucas

bookbub.com/authors/k-lucas

instagram.com/author_klucas

facebook.com/author.klucas

tiktok.com/@klucasauthor

pinterest.com/klucasauthor

twitter.com/AuthorKLucas

READER GROUP

Join the exclusive Facebook reader group!

<u>The Edge of Your Seat Club</u>

HTTPS://WWW.FACEBOOK.COM/GROUPS/

THEEDGEOFYOURSEATCLUB

- Hang out with K. and other fans
- Ask all the questions and start discussions
- Participate in voting and polls
- Enter giveaways
- See behind the scenes
- Talk about your favorite books
- Share memes and humor
- And more!

Looking forward to seeing you there!

ALSO BY
K. LUCAS